The Revolution Begins

Jason Judd

Fourth Printing 2020

All characters, places, or events appearing in this book are fictional, and any resemblance
to real persons, places, or circumstances is not the author's intent.

This book is entirely the work of Jason Judd, this and all previous editions have
had the text and any diagrams intentionally left unedited by others at the
author's request.

"All this happened, more or less."
-K. Vonnegut

J.L.Judd

1.

So J stood there at the bottom the stairs, wondering if he'd be in trouble for sneaking out like he had. His teeth clenched as his head tilted looking up the steps, then down at the floor, then up the steps again. It was dark, and cold. He couldn't see the door above, but he knew it was there. He had lived at this place for over three years now, and had been up and down here only a very few times, at least in his mind; the thought frightened him. Was he getting old? Today he turned thirty years and a half, he was just starting to become afraid of change. He was getting set in his habits, even though the monotony of the last few years in this place he knew had been dreadful. In his mind, J knew that this might be the last time he'd be out in the world for weeks, or even months. His skin felt flushed suddenly, hot, though his fingers were chilled, cold, like he had just handled some Icy-Hot. J swallowed a hard swallow and tried not to think about what lie above. He let the alcohol take a hold and stepped slowly once, twice up the steps, then accepting his fate, he skipped up. The dark, narrow hallway enveloped him like a violent storm at the front of an endless sea.

J reached the top of the stairs, gripped the knob loosely, and slowly turned it trying to remain silent. He pushed the door firmly with his left hand and as the door cracked open, J peered inside the lights were blazing, blinding. He looked across the small kitchen that his door opened to, and into the dining area. Would she be upset? Probably not. But she'd be sure to do everything in her power to make sure he didn't get out again, that he knew. J crossed the threshold of the doorway and the floor of that tiny white kitchen creaked under his feet with every step. J's heart pounded as he moved around the corner of the dining area, he tried to be nonchalant. There she was, as he turned the corner, standing on the polished cherry hardwood. She had some Endust in her left hand, and a clean white rag in the other. She was M. She stopped polishing the small mahogany colored coffee table that sat in front of the wine-colored and forest-green striped couch, and she looked up. She looked disappointed. M pouted, she stomped her right foot softly, and waved her hands up and down quietly.

M was dressed like she always was. She wore a French-maid's uniform, black, with a white lace collar and apron, white lace trimmed her sleeves. M also wore a petticoat beneath her dress that showed beneath her skirt, making the bottom of the costume erect and rigid. She had a white lacey hairpiece too that held her curly, auburn hair back, and out of her eyes. She had on white fishnet stockings that stopped just below where the frilly petticoat showed. You could see the black garter belt that held them up, and there was a fragile white garter with a small black bow around her left thigh, just above her knee. Her skirt was short. At the time that J walked in, M wasn't wearing shoes. Her toenails were polished red and could be seen through the white fishnets that adorned her legs. M set down the rag and dusting chemical that she was holding on to the coffee table in front of her. She softly kicked the leg of the table and curled the toes of her right foot. She clasped her hands together in front of her and J noticed her perfectly manicured fingernails. M had a French manicure—the tips of her nails were polished white.

Though it may seem otherwise, M wasn't really just J's maid, or a high-paid prostitute that J paid to dress up in sexy little outfits and clean his house. To J, she was more than that; the maid, M, was J's captor.

"Where have you been?" M asked quietly, pouting even more deeply. Her voice was sweet. "You know I don't like it when you leave here. It just makes everything seem out of place. Like it's not home anymore."

J then noticed as he glanced around the gleaming room, that the vases, picture-frames, and the decorations, most of which were made of stone, crystal, and brass had all been moved around. The burgundy chair too, where J liked to sit sometimes and read, had been moved away from the large window that opened to the street in front of the loft.

"I know, you don't like it when I leave. Sorry. I just had to, uh…" M stopped J short, pulling him close and kissing him on his cheek.

"Now go in your room, get comfortable, and I'll be there to check on you in a little bit." M ushered J down the narrow hallway to the large bedroom that awaited at its end.

Once inside, J frowned, sighed, sat down on his made bed and held his face in his hands. He heard the door lock behind him. He looked around, there was nothing on the floor. The tall oak dresser was polished. The Burbur carpet was vacuumed, and there was a brown, orange, and white striped afghan neatly folded on the cedar chest at the foot of his bed. On the nightstand to his left, which matched the dresser, there was a half-glass of water, with no ice, and a small blue capsule. J looked at the wall to his right, as he sat on the bed, on which there was a navy blue comforter that was printed with a faint green diamond pattern. The bed had been made so tightly that it barely wrinkled as J set himself on it. He looked at the large rectangular, wooden-framed mirror that hung on the wall across from the doorway; it too, was gleaming, as usual. There were no windows. J pinched the capsule between his right index finger and thumb, placed it deliberately on the back of his tongue, and methodically swallowed the drug down. He laid down on the bed disturbing it a bit. He hadn't changed out of his clothes. He shut his eyes tightly. He drifted off.

2.

A few blocks away, and a few hours earlier, on Kennedy Street, which might as well have been half way around the world, Zeke stepped out into the oncoming evening. He pulled on his windbreaker. He paused for a brief moment and lit a Camel cigarette. Zeke looked around, up and down the street of the small bungalow where he rented out the basement at $200 a month. He pulled up the collar of the tan jacket, zipped up the front, put his hands into the pockets and turned, walking briskly toward Beacon Street, the busiest street that was close enough to easily walk to.

The town could be any in a bustling, suburban area of the northern Midwest; the suburbs of Detroit, Cleveland, Chicago, Indianapolis, they're all the same, but it was here in the small town of Barkley, Michigan, a few miles outside of Detroit, where our story took place. Not much happened in Barkley. It was a safe neighborhood, there was never too much excitement. It was a mere nine miles square, and consisted of lower-middle, to middle class families as well as single people who live alone. Most of the people at this time were white, which was rare in Detroit, even in the suburbs, and they were young, so far as homeowners go. A majority of the houses in the immediate area were built soon after World War I; they started by building small two bedroom, one bath ranches and bungalows. By the 1940's and 50's, some wealthier people started moving into the area, and larger three and four bedroom colonials started going up. Some were quite large, but still, few who lived in Barkley, would ever be considered well enough off to be called even upper-middle class. By the 60's, as Detroit really began to become a metropolis, as the inner city began to become desolate, Barkley had been nearly completely built-up. The larger, wealthier suburbs of Detroit, those farther than a few miles from the city's borders, began to develop. So Barkley'd been there for a while, one of the older suburbs of Detroit.

Zeke didn't mind it there, in Barkley. It was quiet, people kept pretty much to themselves. He knew only one of his neighbors by name: the Hoppers, Tom and Marlene. They were newlyweds, both in their mid to late twenties, who lived in the eight-hundred square foot red-brick ranch style house that was directly to the west of the place where Zeke rented out the basement. He knew them only by their first names though. Tom and Marlene were the only ones that Zeke would ever engage in any conversation of more than just a few civil greetings and retorts. Mr. McManard, the forty-something, single man, who rented Zeke the basement there on Kennedy Street, so close to Beacon Street, was for the past couple of years going through a mid-life crisis. Mr. McManard was rarely home, usually on business trips that took him out of the country, often to Canada, though sometimes to Western Europe, and occasionally to Hong-Kong and Singapore. Mr. McManard was a fairly successful businessman, but found the size of his twelve hundred square foot home appropriate for the lifestyle of a bachelor. McManard frequented the local bars, and when not away on business, spent many nights out, Zeke imagined, with the young ladies that he met at those bars. Zeke would usually see Mr. McManard a mere five or six nights out of the month, and thought that McManard rented out the small basement studio apartment more for the security of knowing somebody was staying there than for profit.

So as the afternoon sun fell, as the birds all began to tuck themselves away into their nests, Zeke headed out down Kennedy Street toward Beacon Street on his way to the Coffee Pot, a coffee shop on the corner of Kennedy and Beacon about a quarter of a mile away. Not five minutes later, as Zeke pulled the last hit off of the second cigarette he had lit during the walk and threw the butt into some bushes in front of the Pot, Zeke pushed open the wooden door adjacent to the large six foot square window behind the bushes and smiled a bit at women who were sitting along the wall to his left. Other than the two women, who were probably both thirty-eight or thirty-nine, and both well groomed and dressed, the place was pretty empty. There was a pretty girl behind the counter who always smiled at Zeke when he was up there at the Coffee Pot. But Zeke didn't pay her much mind. She was probably nineteen years old with a beautiful, full figure; she had the figure of a woman, yet she wore braces still like a little girl. She had shoulder length sandy blonde hair that was pulled back that night amidst a white sun visor. She was wearing a gray Ferris State sweatshirt, and jeans with three large rips in them. They were strategically placed to drive young men to frenzy. Her face was oval, and her nose, buttoned. Her eyes were green that night, though on occasion they were gray. Zeke didn't know her name, he had seen her often, but never asked; he was a private person, he didn't socialize much. The girl, who's name, in fact, was Christine, smiled at him and leaned over the counter next to the register, she looked him straight in his eyes.

"Hi," she said. "How you doin' tonight?"

Zeke managed a nervous, crooked smile. "Oh, I guess I'm alright," he answered in an unassuming, dry and quiet tone.

Christine looked around during the next long moments of silence, holding a soft grin on her slightly parted lips. Zeke could see her braces. "It's pretty cold out there, huh? It's May already for cryin' out loud. Michigan's the worst. It sucks."

Zeke felt uneasy, and the conversation was pretty much one sided. During the talk though, he managed to order a small cup of coffee with a double shot of espresso in it. Christine kept on talking to him as she gave him the cup and he moved to a counter straight across the room from the register. The sugar, cream, stirrer straws and the like were there. Zeke looked down the wall at the two women, who were now laughing cynically about something near the front window. He stirred three teaspoons of sugar into his coffee. Christine asked him if he lived close by, qualifying her question with the fact that she saw him in there quite a bit, but Zeke was not in the mood for conversation and hurriedly made an exit, leaving behind the young Christine, who quickly, upon Zeke's departure, pouted.

3.

J slept for just over two hours—two hours and twelve minutes. He woke up suddenly, his eyes popped open to the dim light given off by the reading lamp that was on the nightstand next to him; he had left it on. His feet were crossed, and his arms were folded across his chest. He realized he hadn't moved at all while he slept, his clothes and the bedspread had barely wrinkled.

J threw his legs over the edge of the bed, sitting up. He straightened his back, stretching some, and wiped his eyes with the fingers of his open hand. He looked around, nothing had changed. The room was desolate as always. There was the nightstand, lit up and to his left; it was nestled between his double bed and the door which was eggshell colored, painted the same as the rest of the room. The tall matching dresser stood on the wall across the room in front of him, and the cedar chest with the afghan on it rested at the foot of his bed. Inside the cedar chest were the clothes that M, J's maid, liked best. They were the only ones that she would normally allow him to wear, if he were lucky enough to be allowed to venture into the family room where he liked to sometimes read. She would be sure to put the acceptable attire in that chest when she approved of it. And when J was permitted to exit the bedroom, M was sure to go into the cedar chest herself and choose the clothing that J was to put on. There were no windows, as has been said, and no closet. J kept the items that he used to keep himself entertained while trapped in the room, either in the nightstand, or in its matching dresser, or under the bed. Lastly, there was the mirror. It hung on the wall opposite the door. It was large and rectangular, and its oak frame too matched the both the nightstand and the dresser. The Burbur carpet was the same eggshell color as the walls except for the hints of royal blue and red that specked it here and there.

J's head spun for a second. The three years of virtual solitude were closing in on him. After all, he liked people. He liked being around them, talking to them, drinking with them. Ever since he hired M though, almost three years ago now to the day, he's been locked away, for what crime, he didn't know. He's thought about it, often wondered what he did to deserve such a fate. He was just looking for a maid, someone to keep the place tidy. It wouldn't be hard, after all, he was neat, he always had been. Without fail, he would put things back where he had found them, he kept his wardrobe clean, and folded. It was just how he was. J was the kind person who showered and shaved twice a day whether he needed to or not. While conducting interviews though, M showed up, in her French-maid outfit, with her hair soft and curled, her small pouty mouth, and big blue eyes—she rarely smiled. She pleaded with J.

M said, "I need this job more than anything I've ever needed before, and if you would be kind enough, and so big-hearted as to hire me, I will watch after you and your house better than you could ever hope for."

J remembered the conversation. She tilted her head downward a little as she looked at him out of the corner of her wide blue eyes, pouting. She was standing with both legs together and straight. She was medium height, about five foot five, with an hourglass body. She was wearing black fishnets that day, and no garter. As she waited for J to say something, she shifted her weight to her left side, lifted her right foot slightly off the ground, batted her long, brown eyelashes, looked down at the ground, which at the that time was dirty in comparison to what it is nowadays, and she fidgeted with the well-manicured fingers that she held in front of her at waist level. J didn't know what to say. He was a bit stunned. He wasn't even expecting anyone when she arrived, and then, there she stood—twenty-two or twenty-three, dressed the part. Beautiful. Her make-up that day, as it has been every day since, was pure artistry, a cross somewhere between a hooker and an angel. J hired her on the spot. Within a few months, M had tidied up so well that J could no longer leave. M would bring him anything and everything he asked for. Don't get me wrong, she loved her boss. She adored him a bit too much.

It all flashed through J's head too fast. He shut his eyes tightly for a brief moment, opened them wide, then sprung up off the side of the bed. He stepped over to the door, turned the knob slowly and pushed. The bolt was locked. J sighed heavily, and was about to knock...

"Do you need something, sweetheart?" M asked quietly, smiling, as she opened the door. "I was waiting for you to wake up. I didn't think you would be able to sleep for very long." Her eyes got wide, so did her grin. "Those little blue pills usually keep you up. I wouldn't think that that'd be that good for you, but everyone keeps telling me to give 'em to you, so I do."

J smiled, he was always nice to her, and to be honest, deep down inside somewhere, there was something that turned him on about being locked up by a pretty girl, dressed as she did, who cleaned his place constantly. She would do anything he asked her to.

"Yeah, they keep me up," he said, and he was about to add that they made him a little nervous, but thought twice about it. No need for M to think he was nervous. "I just need something to drink, M. Please. But no more water, I'm sick of it. I need something sweet. Can't remember the last time I had some orange juice." J could smell it, the orange juice, taste it.

"Don't go anywhere," M said, and before J could turn to sit back down, M arrived back at the door with a half a glass of freshly squeezed orange juice.

J sat on the bed and M set the glass of juice down on the nightstand. She removed the glass that still had some water in it that J had been drinking when he had come home. J thought guilty about sneaking out earlier and was about to mention it to M, and apologize, which would have been his manner, but he stopped himself.

"I think I might need a chair in here, like a Lay-Z-Boy, or maybe a couch. What do you think?"

"Drink your juice, hun." M looked as if J was just kidding. She smiled a crooked little smile, and raised her eyebrows as she looked back at him and left the room. She shut the door.

J waited to hear the door lock, but it didn't. He swallowed his OJ in a few large gulps. His head began to spin. The nightstand against the wall next to the bed took on a glow under the reading lamp that set on it. Then, the bottom drawer began to slowly move, opening. J fell to his knees in front of the piece of small oak furniture, and tried his hardest to hold closed the drawer. He feared he would lose everything that was inside. He rolled over, onto his ass, put his back into the drawer and pushed with his legs. For six minutes he pushed, during the seventh minute he began to sweat. He could push no more. He cried out for M. She was nowhere to be found. J was shoved across the room. He landed flat, palms down, with rug burn on his elbows, hands, and chin. His sweat turned to tears; he was confused, he didn't understand what was happening. He looked up to the mirror that was now in front of him, closing his eyes, he felt tears begin to stream quickly down his face. He wasn't in pain, but his body tensed and contorted as if he was. J forced open his eyes, at the same time he had to open his mouth, the skin on his lips stretched and cracked. Then J felt a chill, and for a few seconds, a few seconds that seemed a few minutes, J couldn't move.

J fell limp, though breathing, his body lay as if it were lifeless.

Slowly, quietly, the door to the bedroom opened a crack. M peered back in. Seeing J, she proceeded to enter the room. M kissed the motionless J leaving hot red lipstick on his cheek. She looked at him, curled up her nose in delight, and pulled the corners of her mouth tight into a happy grin. She was pleased. She methodically started to dust the nightstand, doing what she pleased. She cleaned around J where he lay.

4.

Zeke's clock radio, which was always set exactly eight minutes fast, sounded as it showed 3:35 in stenciled red digits. The blaring revely was an old Velvet Underground song—The Gift. Zeke normally listened to 90.1 FM, the only college radio station that came in on Kennedy Street. The station played classic punk at night. Zeke was more fond of the programming during the afternoons on the station though, for some reason he had a fondness of classical. He was never a musician, and he had never studied music in theory, he was just one of those few people who appreciated the form.

Zeke rubbed his eyes and stretched his jaw as he reached for a Camel on the small table next to him in the dark. He stood, pacing around the small, damp basement room, listening, as Lou Reed told his long tale of the boy who packaged himself up in a box and mailed himself off to his girlfriend. Zeke smiled when Lou got to the end and the girl in the song mistakenly killed the love-starved boy. When The Gift faded into dead air, a habit that 90.1 was occasionally prone to, Zeke stepped over and turned the radio to off.

Zeke smoked his cigarette to the butt, stripped naked and moved to the far end of the small basement where the bathroom was at. He liked his showers hot, almost scalding. He turned on the water and stepped inside; it was a stand-up shower with a glass door, no tub, he closed the door behind him. For twelve minutes the small blue ceramic-tiled bathroom steamed. Zeke grabbed a small white towel he had stolen from a Days Inn on a trip he made to Pittsburgh during the winter. He snatched it intently from a rod on the wall as he opened the shower door, and threw it on the floor in front of him. He dried himself with a second identical towel, and stepped out onto the first. Zeke wiped away the steam from a small circular area on the left hand side of the mirror, and grabbed his face, pulling at his cheeks as he moved his head from side to side. He needed to shave. Quickly he brushed his stained teeth, brushed forward his short dark curly hair, and rolled on some Speed Stick. Zeke left the bathroom door open as he exited it, naked, hoping the room would cool down. Moisture formed on his chest and back as he walked across the dark bedroom. Zeke made his way to the clothes that he had laid out before he laid

J.L.Judd The Revolution Begins

down at 11:30 to go to sleep: black Girbaud jeans, a white T-Shirt from the Banana Republic that Zeke had only worn once before, and white cotton crew socks. He dressed, then fumbled through the closet wondering what he was going to pack. He thought he would probably not be gone for more than the following day and night. He checked his watch, 3:51, and before settling on any wardrobe decisions, Zeke walked back into the bathroom, and shaved, twice, as he always did. In a small, black, nylon bag, Zeke placed a neatly folded pair of blue-jeans, and a black T-shirt which he had never worn; it too was from Banana Republic and he bought it at the same time he bought the white one he was wearing. He put on some black shoes that looked like Doc Martins, even though they weren't, picked his tan wind-breaker off the back of the door that led to the kitchen, thought twice about it, threw it on a reclining chair next to his bed, and pulled a black cotton sport coat from his closet that he had purchased at the Salvation Army. He looked at his watch, it was 4:15. He lit a cigarette, grabbed his keys from beside the clock radio, and pulled from underneath the mattress an envelope containing ten crisp one hundred dollar bills. Zeke counted the money, licked just the tip of the envelope, for some reason he savored the taste of the glue, and sealed it with a swipe of his right index finger and thumb. After tossing the unmarked envelope into the bag on top of his clothes, and zipping the satchel shut, he grasped the short nylon handles of the pack with his left hand. He locked the door as he left. Zeke was methodical, yet precise. He hopped up the five concrete steps that led to the driveway in the back of Mr. McManard's house.

Zeke got into the green Ford Taurus he had rented from a small independent rent-a-car place the preceding morning, and he tossed his bag on the passenger seat. He pulled out of the driveway being sure to drive no faster than 25 mph down Kennedy. He headed toward Beacon Street. Making a left at the corner, Zeke passed the Coffee Pot which was dark at the time but would be opening in less than an hour, and he pulled into a 7-11 about one half mile down the road. He bought a cup of dark-mountain roast for $1.29, and of course, a pack of Camels. Zeke slid back into the Taurus and settled in for the three and a half hour drive to the Essex, a small motel to which he had never been, in Brunswick, near Akron, Ohio.

Zeke drove the speed limit the whole trip: I-75 South, to the Ohio Turnpike, I-80, East, then to I-71, again South. Zeke got off at the Brunswick exit, Exit 79, the Center Road exit, the road that the Essex was nestled on, and headed east. Zeke looked down at the green clock illuminated above the CD player; it said 7:52. About five miles down Center Road, passing Ridge, Zeke noticed a banner stretched high and proud over Center Road announcing that that coming Sunday was Buzzard Sunday, and that there in the town of Hinckley, at Hinckley Elementary School, there would be a pancake breakfast at 7:30. It said the breakfast was sponsored by the Hinckley Chamber of Commerce; that would be the busiest day of the year in Hinckley, Ohio. Every year in that little town, no bigger than five square miles, thousands of people would come from all over the Midwest to celebrate the arrival north of the turkey-vultures, buzzards, if you will. It was a sure sign of spring, and in Hinckley the tradition was nearing a century and a half old. Zeke smiled, and pulled into a church parking lot. Realizing he headed the wrong direction when he got off of I-71, he pulled back out on to Center Road in the forest green Taurus with the rental company's bar-coded bumper, and drove west on the rolling hills beneath the freeway. Zeke passed under I-71 at 35 mph, and traveled two more miles before coming to the Essex which sat on the south side of Center Road.

Zeke pulled into the lot. He parked not near the motel, but closer to the street. He opened the packet of cigarettes he had bought back at the 7-11 on Beacon Street. Seeing that he had already smoked nearly half of them, he closed the box back up, and tossed it on the coin tray beneath the radio, next to the empty coffee cup, and in front of the gearshift. He sighed. The clock said 8:09. Zeke looked at his watch, it read 8:18. He looked around the cab of the car, not for anything in particular, it was just a long drive, and he had only stopped once, about forty-five minutes south-east of Toledo. Zeke managed to gather himself, realizing he had only gotten around four short hours of sleep, and that that was not quite enough. He got out of the Taurus and stretched his neck, tilting his jaw to the left and grabbing the muscle at the nape of his neck with his right fingertips. He walked casually around to the passenger side of the sedan. Opening the door, he reached in for his the black jacket which he had removed when he stopped after passing through Toledo, slipped into it, grabbed the small bag, removed it from the car, and shut the door. His hand never left the framing of the window on the door. He pressed it closed as a valet properly would. Zeke popped the trunk by pressing the tiny blue button in the bottom right corner of the already small, oddly shaped key fob. The button had a small white diagram of the rear of a car, it's trunk open. After gently placing the bag in the trunk and closing the latter, Zeke slipped his hands into the pockets of his coat, put his head down, and looking at the ground, he walked across the gravel ridden parking lot to the small office beneath the large, and always well-lit sign that read Essex Motel.

"Howdy," the shrinking old man behind the desk said, putting down his paper. "What can I do ya for?" He smiled.

"Been driving all night," Zeke sighed. "Came in early for Buzzard

Sunday," he said with a smile as he remembered the banner over in Hinckley.

"Oh, will do," the old man said clicking the back of a ballpoint pen and shuffling around some pages in a book on the desk. "What d'ya need, single? Double?"

"Better give me a double, I'm hoping to meet a buddy of mine here. He's coming from Pittsburgh, goes by the name of Rob. If he comes in looking for me, could you please tell him what room I'm in? My name's James, James Morris." Zeke looked at the key the old man handed him, and Zeke gave the man forty dollars from his wallet. The old man offered Zeke no change. "Room 219. Thanks." Zeke reiterated as he left the office. He climbed a rusty flight of stairs that were once painted white, and walked along the balcony to room 219.

After fighting with the lock for a few seconds, Zeke opened the door surveying the scene. The beds were made and clean, there were fresh towels, the floor had been vacuumed. He turned on the television with the remote that was bolted to the stand between the beds, and walked over to the window. He pushed to the side the heavy pink curtain and peered out—nothing but an empty Center Road. It was quiet.

5.

About the same time that Zeke was checking in to room 219 at the Essex, in Brunswick, Ohio, J, back in Barkley, up in his loft, a couple of blocks from Kennedy Street, was waking up to breakfast in bed: complements of M. She was bringing him a toasted bagel sandwich with three eggs and a pile of fried ham on it. J felt good, delightful. Then he flashed back to the fish-out he had done the evening before. He had been out for quite a while, nearly nine hours; M in her cleaning had carried him to bed.

M set down the brass breakfast tray which was polished to a mirror-like finish. There was coffee, and milk, no juice that morning.

"And how are you this morning, fine sir?" M posed, shaking her shoulders sinuously as she set the tray down.

"This looks good," is all J replied to her. He was looking around the room slowly, taking inventory of every detail. All was quite the same; somehow though, the mirror seemed larger, bigger than it was in reality.

J's smile became wide, and his stare, though it saw something, was not focused as he looked toward the mirror. J picked his head up quickly towards M, tightening his smile, and squinting his eyes; he waited for M to say something. He wondered how he'd gotten to bed.

M gracefully touched the tip of J's nose with her left index finger, whispered something to J that he couldn't understand, and then the maid gave him a quick peck on the cheek. Just coming to reality, J then realized that M wasn't wearing her black vest with the white buttons, or the black skirt. M was simply wearing her white lace petticoat, and lace undershirt; the shirt was black lace with short, sheer white sleeves. She had on white thigh highs, and a red and white garter on her left thigh. The sides of her curly auburn hair were pulled up to the top of her head, and tied with a black ribbon that hung down to her shoulders, over her neck, to the top of her spine, the length of her hair. M said nothing, she just smiled the smile of an eighteen-year-old girl on spring break somewhere, at a beach, hardly dressed, up in a hotel room. She fidgeted with her manicured fingernails that had white tips. She tilted her head, still smiling. The moment was long relative to J.

"Do you need to tell me something? You look like you need to ask me something. What's goin' on?" J honestly wondered.

"Well it's just that," M sat on the bed, all in her black and white lace, putting her hands on her knees with her elbows straight. She curled her toes, and batted her eyes as she gazed at his; she pouted. "It's Friday, and I hate to bother you about it, but I was wondering if I could get paid in cash this week."

"Whatever makes you happy, Dear." J mumbled, sighing.

"Thank you sooooo much," M said, touching his nose again with the point of her finger, "You can't even imagine how much I appreciate it." She smiled curtly.

J managed an amorous, childlike smile. M turned and left, purposely pushing out her left hip, and swaying slowly, in J's face, her ass. J looked at the back of M's bare thighs: the gap between the top of her stockings and the bottom of her petticoat. J's face took back that lost and unfocused blank stare as M walked out. She didn't look back, and J heard the bolt on the door lock as M shut it.

He had lost his appetite. As he looked at the egg sandwich next to him, he opened the bottom drawer of the oak nightstand next to him, and removed two crisp hundred dollar bills, a slightly worn fifty, three twenties, and two tens; that was how M liked to be paid. He laid the money on the nightstand where she would be able to see it the next time she came in. He paid her in cash every Friday, and didn't understand why every week she insisted on asking him the question that, just before, she asked. M would always go out to get more cash, unless a request for J's presence came formally from the bank in the mail, then she would let him go. One of the first things she did once she was hired was have her name put on J's savings account; so she could pay the bills. M made J pay for everything in cash. All his bills; gas, electric, mortgage, water: everything. M would take J's cash, all dressed to please, up to the local 7-11 on Beacon Street, where she would have money orders made in the amounts that were to be paid.

A valet would sometimes come from a valet company that J retained at the request of M, and a different teenage boy would show up at her request for occasional work. They would get money orders made, as was said, and they would go to the grocery, and the drug store. And they would buy cigarettes for M. And sometimes, they would go to the nutrition and health food store to buy several supplements on a doctor's advice, things which none of them could pronounce, and bring them back for J. Everything was paid for in cash. J paid the valet, $80 a day, cash. So once a month, or if an emergency came up, M went to the bank, with a large, khaki-colored, canvas bag, and make a cash withdrawal that would be sufficient for the month, or likewise, appropriate for an emergency.

M would return to the loft with the bag; up the dark stairs she would go, through the kitchen, and through the dining room, and she would hurry into J's bedroom and lock the door behind. J would then count the money M had withdrawn, just as if he were at the bank, and neatly place it, organized by the bills' denominations, in the bottom drawer of the pale, oak nightstand next to his tightly made bed.

J's appetite grew a little again, he picked up his brass breakfast tray and began eating the sandwich. He sipped the dark coffee, and grabbed the little blue capsule that rolled out from beneath the white paper plate that the sandwich was on. He placed the pill on the back of his tongue and drank down the entire glass of milk, he crushed the 12 oz. styrofoam cup that the 2% with the blue cap had been poured into, then he continued to sip on his coffee; it was just how he liked it, dark and bitter with plenty of sugar.

He looked up, down the length of his bed, across the room; on the wall, the mirror was bigger than ever, distorted, it wavered. Like a cold lake, in early spring, in mid-Michigan, it waved. J heard a thumping sound, over and over again, rhythmically, -1- -2- 1- -2-. The dull gray of the silvered glass began to shine bright, white, phosphorous burning white. And from the light, J saw come from the glass, a cactus. It was green and shining, and as it came toward him, it opened, splitting apart into two length-pieces. Inside, the cactus was red. Inside, amidst the red, there was a sphere, a black shiny pearl of a sphere. J reached for the medicine.

The door opened with a slam. J jerked his head toward M; she stood there with a half a glass of water, and a black tablet, round and smooth, on a red ceramic plate. The pill was about one-quarter of an inch in diameter, scored into quarters, a -B- was imprinted on one side, a -C- had been imprinted on its reverse.

"Medicine from the stony earth." J heard a deep voice mumble. The voice retained authority. J looked at the mirror quite in a scare. Time stopped. Then he looked back at the tablet. Back and forth his eyes and head darted. J did not quite know what to do.

"Take it," the mirror suggested boldly. "Take it and I will show you the way. I will unlock for you the mystery of your reflection."

J looked away from the larger-than-life mirror, he glanced at the black dot on the red plate, then he looked up at M. She was smiling. She seemed oblivious, unknowing of the life that had been taken by the mirror. J plucked the black pill with his right index finger and thumb, as the other three fingers on the hand clenched. He tossed the tablet far into the back of his throat. He gripped the half glass of water then with the same hand and swallowed the medicine quickly.

"I know you'll like that," M squealed, as J pulled at her skirt, she was now in her full uniform. M turned, looking into the mirror. She tussled her hair with her right hand, and held it in place with her left. She blew a kiss toward her reflection, her left eye winking slowly, delicately, the only tension in her face was on her lips, and that left, winking eye. She turned quickly in the direction opposite of J. She made sure to expose her ass to him. She didn't even look his way though as she shut the door. The bolt however, she left unlocked. She had been doing that more and more lately. Maybe she was ready for some company out in the room where M sometimes permitted J to read, in front of the large window that opened to the street just a couple blocks from Kennedy.

J laid back and looked at the mirror, frightened again. But the mirror was just a mirror: a normal rectangular sheet of silvered-glass, about three-and-a-half feet in height, and two-and-a-half feet across, framed in a beveled white oak frame. J scratched over his left brow and dug in his right ear to where an itch had moved to. Then he stretched forward his back. He put his hands on his knees. Then he swung his legs off the side of the bed, and looked again into the glass.

J was wearing blue nylon soccer shorts with white circles on them, a triangle was on the front, on the bottom-left. He had no hair on his body except for on his head, and that was dark and very short, a new millennium, conservative-style business look. He had no facial hair, except for eyebrows which were so thin you couldn't see them unless you closely examined him. J had striking facial features, and he was thin, yet naturally strong. He was dark all around; he was told that he had three lines of Native American blood in him; two of his sixteen great-great-grandparents had been of the seven nations of Iroquois; he wasn't sure which. And J also had some Powhatan blood in his veins, old blood, from the 17th century. It is unimportant, but J was, in fact, a direct descendent of Pocahontas. Legally though, and culturally, J was Caucasian. His skin was usually dark as fresh cherry, but being so early in the spring, he had not yet colored.

J looked up and down the mirror. It appeared normal. Then his reflection said aloud to him, "Time."

6.

Zeke spent a majority of the day that he arrived at the Essex observing everything that made up its environment. He saw one maid during that day; she was pushing a cart that had folded white linens and towels on it, with a canvas hamper attached to its front full of dirty laundry. The maid was a young white girl, she had just turned nineteen, and having run away from home at the age of fourteen, she never finished high school and was happy to be making the nine dollars an hour that she was. She went from empty room to empty room, taking her time, freshening the places up for the next drifters who were to come stay at the old motel. She didn't bother Zeke; he was edgy that day, but her innocent, unpolished, girl next-door face brought a smile to his cheeks the couple of times he saw her. She asked him sweetly if he needed anything. Zeke told her he just needed some rest, hoping she would stay away from him, but something about her, whether it was pheromones, or maybe she reminded Zeke of a girl he knew at some point years before, made his stomach turn. Zeke did his best to avoid her which wasn't that difficult a task. He made a couple of trips down to the office on the north side of the building to check on the old man, ask him if he had received any news from Rob, but really Zeke was just trying to get a fix on what went on around the place. The old man in the office was always reading: a newspaper from Akron, a newsletter from Brunswick, and an old novel, Indian Summer, by John Knowles. The lot, which had only four cars in it when Zeke arrived that morning, had seven in it by a quarter to six that evening. Zeke saw one man who checked in. He looked down on his luck, his wife had just thrown him out. Nothing notable really happened, at least as far as Zeke could tell, at the Essex that day. At six o'clock, when Zeke picked up the phone in the room to make a call, which he put on his Visa, the forty-two-room motel was pretty empty, just six rooms were rented. The phone was affixed to the table between the beds, right beside the likewise secured remote.

"Rob?" Zeke asked as he heard someone pick up the other end.

"Yeah, it's me." A whiny, stressed voice answered. Rob was expecting the call, it was six o'clock, right on time. "What's goin' on? Everything cool?" Rob was pretty relaxed. He was a graduate student at The Ohio State University studying nuclear engineering.

"Everything's fine, man. I'm here, at the beautiful Essex Motel, in lovely Brunswick, Ohio. How do you handle it in this state? You drink a lot?" Zeke had a serious tone in his voice.

"Just study, man, you know me. Come on, how long have we known each other?" Rob sounded as if he really needed a friend. He didn't really care if Zeke was taking advantage of him, Rob just liked being useful for something.

"It's been a while," Zeke answered with a quiet chuckle remembering how everyone used to talk behind Rob's back at Johnson Middle School, where the two had met nearly twenty years before. "So you got what I asked you for, right?"

"I got it. You'd better not get busted, this could get us both into some serious shit. What the hell you need this stuff for anyway? There's not enough of it to really do anything that exciting with it." Rob was curious.

"I just met this guy, and he had this theory… anyway… don't worry about it. I'll explain it all to you later. You'll find out, one way or another at some point." Zeke looked out the window of the room, a bit nervous. He was calm though, for what was about to go down. Maybe he just didn't fully understand. "So how long 'til you get here? Where you at?"

"I'll get there, just relax, in about forty-five minutes or so." Rob took on an air of calm. He really didn't fully understand what was going to happen either.

"Room 219, man. And if you run into the old man in the office, I checked in by the name Morris, James Morris, but you know, just avoid him if you can. I've known you a long time, man, and I know you're cool enough to do this without asking too many questions, even though it's a little crazy. You're cool that way man, but I'm gonna take care of ya, you just can't let anyone know anything about this. Ever. We straight?" Zeke's eyes were wide. He grinned. He was stressed.

"Room 219, man. Just relax. I'll be there. You're not gonna get into any trouble, are you?" Rob tried to assure himself. He was picking up on Zeke's excitement.

Zeke just laughed on the other end. "I'll see you in a few, man."

"Right." Rob clicked off his cell phone.

So there was Rob, Robert N. Himer to be exact, driving north on I-71 in his beat up 1986 Toyota Celica, on his way to meet an old friend, a friend that he had known for over half of his life, with seven grams of Plutonium-239 which he had reacted himself at OSU, in Columbus. He was getting his Ph.D. in nuclear engineering. He was a brilliant student, and everyone there at The Ohio State University loved him. He had a key to the lab. He knew no one would ever know anything about what happened; no one even really knew what he did in there. He spent eighteen, nineteen hours a day in that lab, and to anyone other than him, and soon Zeke, the Plutonium sample he had made never even existed. For Rob, it was really that easy; it's frightening, Pu-239.

Rob couldn't even figure out why Zeke had even asked him for it, the Plutonium. To make a bomb, you need upwards of fifteen pounds of the stuff. It all seemed pretty harmless to Rob, he had reacted only seven grams of it. He wasn't even thinking twice about it as he pulled into the parking lot of the Essex Motel fifty-two minutes later. He looked down at the dash and noticed his tank was almost on "E". It was a long drive from Columbus to Akron, and he smiled, knowing he was going to hit Zeke up for some gas money. Rob grabbed the small, lead-lined, hard rubber tube like those he often used to store highly active samples in. It was definitely necessary, as the stuff he had made for Zeke was just under 94% pure, but not quite weapons grade. Zeke had asked for something fissionable with a purity upwards of 97%, but in the six weeks that Zeke had given him, 94% was the best Rob could do. He snatched his cell-phone off of the passenger seat, and grabbed the heavy, black, lead, and rubber tube away from the ashtray. The case was about the size of a Plen-T-Pack of gum. He opened the car door, and it did as it always did; it seemed as if it was about to fall off. He was sure that one day it would, just plummet to the street with the handle still in his hand, but not today. Rob got out of the car, slipping the phone in the left pocket of his khaki pants. His white button-down shirt had pastel stripes on it, the top three buttons were undone. He realized the clothes he was wearing were baggy, too baggy to conceal something the size of a pack of gum, weighing over a quarter of a pound; it was lead. So Rob just clutched the large, heavy capsule tightly in his right hand and looked around the barren parking lot, then glancing over his shoulder across the street, he headed quickly for the rusted, white, steel staircase. "Room 219," he muttered under his breath, as he looked at his steel watch. It was five minutes to seven.

Rob knocked three times as he tried to peer through the rusted screen of dirty window. Zeke popped his head through the pink curtains, a big smile on his face. Rob held up the small black case that he was still holding in his right hand, and waved with his left hand, boldly, and with a single motion, likewise, to his left. He smiled, and began to laugh. He hadn't seen Zeke in a couple of years. Zeke peered side to side out the window as a blank look drew across his face. He disappeared behind the curtains, and Rob heard the bolt of the door

J.L.Judd   The Revolution Begins

turn. Zeke's dark head slowly emerged as the door opened. Again, he peered from side to side. Zeke then opened the door wide, and held open his arms to give Rob a hug.

The deal went down as Zeke had hoped: like nothing was even going on. And Rob explained that the Plutonium had never even existed to anyone who would make a fuss about it, "It's like I run the place," he said. "Don't get me wrong. Security's tight, if you're not supposed to be there. But that reactor, it's like I live there. By the end of the summer, I'll be Dr. Himer."

Zeke forced Rob to take the grand that he had brought along for him for his trouble. Rob laughed a little, after all, he did need some gas money, so the cash was a nice surprise, as getting an unexpected grand always is. They talked for a couple of hours, the whole while Zeke proved to be quite elusive about why he needed the Plutonium. Rob didn't really press the issue. The two of them just caught up on old times; Zeke filled Rob in on the happenings around Barkley, MI. Rob realized he was happy to be gone, out of dreary Barkley as they decided to leave the Essex and get a drink, and some food. Zeke hadn't eaten all day. Zeke was sure to take the small black case with the Plutonium sample and secure it inside the spare tire deep within the trunk of his rental car. It seemed something only people smuggling drugs would think of. The two ate at a bar about four and a quarter miles from the motel. The old man in the Essex's office had pointed them in that direction; the place was called The Fat Man, and the food was good, but greasy. They ate well. They ordered fried mushrooms, and fried cheese, half-pound burgers, onion rings and fries. They split a pitcher of Budweiser. The whole time, Rob was quietly trying to figure out what Zeke was up to. He was quite intrigued, curious. But Zeke never let Rob in on it. Zeke was just happy he'd gotten what he was looking for, and it was all so easy.

7.

For two and a half days, J laid on his bed, in his own cold sweat, quivering. He had forgotten about the black tablet M had given him. He remembered M peaking her turned-up little nose through the occasional crack in the door. M never said anything though those two and a half days; J would simply hear the bolt on the door slide open, then it would open a crack, and then would appear M's gleaming eyes, peering into the badly lit room. The small reading lamp was lit. It was on the nightstand, that piece of furniture next to the bed that had, in the eyes of J, taken such a presence just a few short days before, as did the mirror more recently. Or was it weeks ago? J didn't remember, time had abruptly lost its place in J's head. The nightstand did, though, frighten J. He was terrified of it; lying there in his dripping, icy sweat. He had not forgotten about the mirror, but as of that point, he could hardly relate any malice to the silvered glass itself, he more feared the reflection in it.

He stayed in bed, and as M would occasional make her visits to the door, J's big, wide eyes would hurriedly lose their fix on the dimly lit nightstand next to him, and focus on the jarred door. He would try to speak, scream, make any kind of noise at all with his voice every time M would appear, but he couldn't. He was in most senses of the word—paralyzed. Without sleeping for those two and a half days, or was it a week, for each appearance of M, and as he tried to call out for her, he prayed for her emergence through that door. And the door began to take on its own immortality, at least in J's mind.

Occasionally, he would see the door open. He would try to call out, sweating, eyes wide, unable to move, and nothing would appear, not even M. It would swing open, and then again closed, as if something, or nothing, was checking on him. This happened infrequently at first, but as the second day approached the third, and J had not slept, not even for a moment, this strange occurrence began to happen more and more; and the appearance of M's glimmering eyes through a mere crack, less and less. Then after two and a half days of this, the door was opening wide with the frequency of the clock in the other room chiming, a chime which J had never noticed before, and as J's mouth began to open, as he tried to yell, or scream, or call out to M, or to anyone who would listen, someone emerged through the door.

J squinted, and he rubbed the sweat from his eyes. The icy cold he perspired, gave way to a tingling heat, and he knew, somewhere deep inside, that what was happening wasn't real, but it was. It was happening. J focused his eyes as his damp fingers slipped from his face, and he knew then he could see someone. Someone was coming through the door. It was...

"Dad!" J managed to scream, in a dull hollow scream that penetrated the walls of the loft.

M continued to clean; she straightened the new, mahogany grandmother clock she had hung on the wall early that afternoon on the wall across from the window where J sometimes liked to read.

J's father looked warmly upon his child, and his eyes filled with tears. He wept, and J screamed again, a dreadful, hollow scream that resonated from deep within his throat. J held out his arms, and tried to speak. His lips quivered, and salty sweat flowed quickly then into his left eye. He reached for the stinging eye with his clammy right hand, and his Father, still weeping, then reached for him. With his right arm extended, the figure reached for J. J swallowed a hard swallow, the kind that hurts a throat. It made him cough, then choke. Upon hearing the noise, J's father reached with his other arm and wept harder. J then wailed; it sounded of agony.

M threw down the clean white rag she was dusting with, frustrated. Her face scowled, but atop her uniform, the short black dress, and lace petticoat, and white fishnet thigh-highs that she was dressed in, the scowl looked more a pout. And she walked quickly down the hall that led to J's room, and she unbolted the door, and she peered in.

J squinted his eyes, rubbing them. His father was no longer there, he saw M's eyes gazing coldly at him. J cried aloud. Like a baby in pain, J cried. The door flung open.

"What is wrong with you?" M demanded.

J was able finally to form a word, "Is...? Is...?"

M stepped toward him and with her hand she wiped the sweat from his forehead.

J's wide-open mouth began to quake. M knelt beside the bed, and she kissed him softly. J cried even louder. M pouted as she stood, and she threw down her arms in defiance as she turned and left the room. J eyed the open door. He tried to get up off the bed, but managed only to get his left leg on the floor. M ran back in, and pulled J from the bed. J could see that M was carrying a long, thin, blue and yellow box. He cried in joy as she pulled him to his feet.

J saw M pull the plastic wrap from the box. And then she wrapped. Around him, again, and again, the cellophane gripped him tighter with each turn. She began around his arms before J could even think of defying her, for it wasn't something that he normally would do. He was trapped, entombed in the shrunken plastic. J tried to move, first his arms, then his legs; he couldn't. M pushed him down when she was through wrapping J in her cocoon; and falling on the floor, J realized he had stopped crying. M climbed on top of him. She leaned over to kiss him, and J woke up. He had fallen asleep after all.

J looked around the empty, dimly lit room. He looked at the nightstand next to the bed, and then at the door which opened a crack after he heard the bolt slide open, and he saw M's eyes peer through the sliver of light which shone through the door. The door opened.

"You're finally awake!" M rejoiced. "It's been three days. Now here." M set down a half a glass of water on the nightstand, and a familiar blue capsule next to it. She leaned over and kissed J on the cheek softly. "You're sweating," she said.

J said nothing. He reached over and pinched the capsule in the fingers of his shivering right hand, and he swallowed it slowly. He watched the door close behind M as she left the room, and the bolt slid locked behind her. Then realizing he couldn't move, J tried to scream, but couldn't.

J.L.Judd

8.

The next few weeks were uneventful for Zeke, for the most part. Most notable of events, was his inability to sleep. Zeke would fall asleep quite well, and on a good schedule; he would be asleep between one and one half hours before midnight. But about four nights a week, Zeke would wake up at 3:30 am, on the nose. The other three days, out of the week, Zeke would finally manage to drag himself out of the bed, in his small basement studio apartment at Mr. McManard's on Kennedy Street, at noon. He wasn't working, he had quit his job at Barkley Rare and Used Books just before he had made his trip to Brunswick.

It was early in the morning, 3:33, three weeks to the day after Zeke had returned home from Ohio. Zeke was awake; he had just opened his eyes and was alert, he knew he was not going to be able to fall back to sleep. Zeke rolled over to the right side of his Queen sized bed, reached for a cigarette that was on the small round table there and lit it. He exhaled, lifting his eyes toward the ceiling, being careful not to disturb the thick streamline plume that was emitted from the cigarette. He looked around, the dark room was clean, and organized, not too much decoration. A plastic vase and a wooden jar stood on the nightstand and the dining table respectively. There were fake flowers in the vase on the left side of the bed, and real flowers, daffodils, which he had cut from Mr. McManard's garden, in the painted jar where Zeke ate. And there were a few candles here and there, randomly set at places which necessity had dictated. The carpet was a cold, dark blue. It was the color of the North Atlantic during Halloween. The walls were painted a gray that could pass for purple. There was wooden two-inch molding around the edges of the ceiling. The molding was stained a dark oak. Zeke glanced around as he adjusted to the scarce light in the room. His bathroom light was on, the door was ajar. He decided he needed something on the walls: paintings, posters. He could barely see the couch across the room from his bed, the couch itself and the lighting were both too dark. He could though, see the white vertical stripes of the afghan that was folded over the sofa's back.

Zeke got out of bed, he was wearing navy cotton shorts that had a gray stripe down each side. They were long, they stretched almost to his knees, and they were made from sweats, cut off and hemmed at the bottom. He bumped into the stereo rack, as he rolled off the right side of the bed, and rubbed his right knee for a moment. Zeke ran his fingers through his hair as he walked around the base of the bed, along the couch. Then he lit a candle on the table that he always had set with clean dishes, a single place setting. He smoked his cigarette wondering what to do. He was running out of things to do at 3:30 in the morning. He looked around some more, and thought that the small safe under the bed, which he could see from where he sat at the table, looked out of place. It was really the only thing that had changed in the place since he had moved in. He had bought the safe upon his return from Ohio when he visited Rob, now he didn't think he really needed it. He liked his environment plain, simple, undistracting. He forgot about the paintings and posters. He didn't even have a television set. He thought they filled too many hours with futility. He knew he would have to find a more inconspicuous place for the safe. Later.

Zeke got dressed, he put on some old, torn jeans, a blue T-shirt that said "BAD BOY" on it in white stencil letters, and some black sandals. The shirt was from a T-shirt shop down on Beacon Street. Zeke brushed his teeth and his hair, and put on the black wire framed glasses that he seldom wore. He paced around a bit, glancing over one of a few shelves of paperbacks he had along the wall in a small alcove, across from the dining table, past the stereo, to the left of his bed. The alcove housed the bathroom door. Then realizing he was getting fidgety, at a few minutes past 4:00 that morning, Zeke walked back across the room, past the rack of stereo equipment, between the bed and the couch, over to the table where he blew out the candle. He then walked through the narrow archway, into and through the small kitchen, and out the door. He bounced up the few concrete steps and grabbed his green, ten-speed, Fuji racing bike from Mr. McManard's garage, and whipped along Kennedy Street to Beacon. There was no traffic. As he made a left at the Coffee Pot, he wiped some sweat from his forehead, he knew it was going to be hot. It was the first week in June, in Michigan, and it was humid. The last three days had broken ninety degrees Fahrenheit. Zeke let go of the handlebars and pedaled about a half a block down Beacon Street. He leaned over and turned the bike across the street as he looked over his shoulder. He pedaled about another hundred yards, and right before the 7-11 turned into the parking lot of a small diner, or coney island, as they're called in Detroit, that was open twenty-four hours. Zeke locked his bike with a long padlock that hooked the spokes of his front wheel to the forks, and he went inside.

The place was pretty empty. There was one old man eating scrambled eggs, bacon, and white toast at the counter. There was a petite brunette waitress. She was wearing no make-up, and her hair was coarse and unkempt, but she was pretty. She was twenty-five or twenty-six. She was wearing a short jean skirt, and a pink sleeveless cotton shirt, and a short, black apron hung from her waist in front. And there was an old Lebanese man who could be seen in the kitchen wearing white-cotton clothes, a black baseball hat, and a greasy gray apron.

Zeke sat down at a small booth made for two and looked out the window. The girl came over and poured Zeke some coffee. He ordered pancakes and hash browns. Zeke did not make small talk. He had become reclusive since his trip to see Rob, and the days like these were lonely and boring. Zeke ate his breakfast, doing his best to ignore the waitress when she would come to fill his coffee, and gossip. She was as bored and as lonely as Zeke was. In realizing that Zeke wasn't up for meaningless conversation, she let him pretty much eat in peace and tried to talk politics with the old man at the counter: the usual—peace, war, jobs, money, that kind of thing. Zeke tuned them out and began to focus on a kid using the payphone across the street that ran perpendicular there to Beacon, at the 7-11. The kid was about nineteen or twenty, thin, with a green and red, spiked haircut. He was wearing army surplus pants from the Vietnam era, and a black t-shirt with the sleeves cut off. The kid had a chain on his wallet that was clipped to his pants, and black Doc Martin boots. As Zeke ate, the kid talked on the phone; during which time a car, a white VW Jetta pulled up. The driver of the Jetta got out of his car and before going into the convenience store to get a cherry Slurpee, he talked to the punked out kid who was on the phone. They shook hands, passed something between them, and Zeke saw them exchange a couple of dollars. Zeke finished off his pancakes as the Jetta pulled away. He left eight dollars on the table for the $4.98 bill with a $3.02 tip and walked out of the small restaurant. Behind the building he unlocked the front wheel of his bike, hopped on, and pulled around the front of the restaurant towards 7-11. The kid was still there.

Zeke looked at his watch, it was 4:50. He looked around and there was no traffic. He pulled up on his bike in front of the kid who still had not hung up the phone.

"Waz up?" Zeke hissed.

The grungy kid looked up at Zeke. "You're out here awfully early," he said articulately.

"You know me, I'm out here early quite a bit." Zeke's eyes were glassy, he was excited. "Just need two. I got ten on it." Zeke pulled a ten-dollar bill from his right, front pocket, handed it to the kid on the phone, who in return gave Zeke two small squares of paper. It was LSD.

"You know you should stay away from this stuff," the dealer said to Zeke. "You know, if you get caught with LSD, you can be charged with conspiracy to overthrow the government. It's like treason or something."

Zeke just smiled, and laughed, then he waved as he sped away on his green Fuji racing bike. He loved starting these days out with a nice long bike ride. He rode eight miles that morning.

9.

J looked around the barren room. It was cool for that time of year, but the room's lack of windows left a stale taste in the air. J was getting lonely. M would come in occasionally to give him his pill, and sometimes some food which he rarely ate, but she scarcely said more than two words to J. J passed the days and nights alone for the most part. Day after day, for the next few weeks J sat by himself, with his eggshell colored walls, freshly vacuumed carpeting, and tightly made bed, of which the headboard matched the other polished wooden furniture in the room; and now there was that damned chiming of the grandmother clock, which J had not yet seen. It was such a sad reminder to J of each sterile hour that passed.

J's dreams began to get worse. They were coming to him now occasionally while he was awake. A figure often spoke to him from the mirror, that large mirror with the polished oak frame. The figure was merely an outline, like a cartoon, a yellow outlined cartoon of a head, a man's face that spoke to J. The figure's voice was harsh yet comforting. J quickly concluded that the figure must be God. Now to J, this is how God appeared; the details of his dress were ambiguous, as when J would try to recall them specifically, he couldn't, but J could remember that God was always dressed, at least as well as a yellow sketch can be. Sometimes He would wear a suit of sketched clothes, or from time to time, his clothes would appear as real as any J had ever seen anyone wearing. God sometimes wore a double-breasted jacket, and He sometimes wore a raincoat. J never paid great attention to the specifics of God's clothes. God's head though, J recalled with great detail; He had a head of full, thick, curly hair, more a bronze than a yellow. He had great wrinkles across his brow that moved as He scolded J and told him how things were, and should be. His eyes bulged. They were wide and bloodshot, at least as bloodshot as a yellow sketch can be. God's nose was large, straight and pointed; J recalled that it reminded him of his father's. And God's lips were full and wide, and when He appeared to J, always moving. God would tell J things, about the future, about how things would be; He said over and over again that He was just getting to know J, that He had a secret to reveal to him, a very important secret, and that, as God should, He just had to make sure that J was ready for such a secret.

God would joke with J, show him great visions of a sky full of white billowy clouds across the ceiling. He would show J visions of beautiful women that would one day make his acquaintance. J would get very excited, his mind drifting from his solitude, and the chiming of the clock. However, when M would unbolt the door from the outside, and open it slowly to see J standing in front of the mirror, God would go away. J would turn to her, and in his state of euphoria as he was just speaking to God, he quickly became quite taken with M's beauty.

He would take her hand and kiss it softly after she would set J's blue capsule and half glass of water on the nightstand. M would blush, for there was something different about J these days, maybe it was the way he smelled, she didn't know, but she too was being taken by him. For nearly four weeks this went on; J would talk to God until M would enter the room, she would give him his pill, and blush at his compliments, not knowing how to react. Then after four weeks of this, a small scored yellow table began to join the blue capsule and the half glass of water. M had heard J speaking to God. She had been blushing out of fear, and anxiety. All she wanted to do was to help J, her master, her boss.

J rested for the next couple of weeks, alone. God was gone, for the moment, but the introduction had been made, J thought to himself, and perhaps if J was the one God was looking for, he'd be back. In the meantime, J's new obsession with his maid, always dressed up in her cute little uniform, and baring a soft pouty grin, only meaning to J that she adored him to his deepest bone, had become quite insatiable.

The silence that came with the little yellow tablet was isolating. The dreams were gone and all J could think of were the beautiful women that God had shown to him. J needed a friend, and M knew it.

J woke up softly. He was lying on the left side of the bed, the side closest to the door, his weight on his right side. His eyes opened to the sight of M sliding into the bed next to him. J felt it was a dream. It had to be. He dared not move. His eyes widened as M turned her head toward him, her eyes then met his. M smiled, it was a warm, pleasant smile. Her soft, curled hair was twisted high on her head, and she wore a merlot-colored silk camisole that hugged her body with testosterone-producing precision. Her skin was lightly, yet evenly tanned—bronzed, and her figure was soft and beautiful, not being held tightly in her petticoat. J studied her carefully in astonishment. He had not seen her out of her uniform in eighteen months, and on that occasion M had worn jeans and a sweater. That was the night M had found him out at a bar, sickly drunk; it was a night that he had escaped. J didn't remember it well, but he could recall what M was wearing. She wasn't a maid that night. She dragged him out of the bar, took him home, and took care of him.

M lay back on the bed, on top of the covers. She leaned back on her elbows, looking at J. Her soft, bare legs were bent at the knees as she curled her painted toes and twisted her ankles so her two big toes almost touched. M tilted back her head, looking up at the white ceiling. She giggled, her round breasts shook. M straightened out her legs and bent over forward at the waist as if she was trying to touch her toes. She held her head up, and sighed. M looked at J again, she tilted her head to the right slightly, and reaching across her body with her right arm. M touched J on his hip, curled up her nose, pulled herself against him, and fell asleep.

J was scared stiff. He couldn't move. He dared not touch her. What if she didn't approve? He didn't know why she was doing this. What would happen if he kissed her? If he pulled her close? Would she think he was trying to rape her? J couldn't bare such a thought. This was all new. So he laid there that night, a night that would not soon repeat itself, stiff as a board, eyes wide, staring at M, smelling her sweet breath, watching the breath fill and then leave her lungs as she quietly slept, like an angel. M knew what J needed.

J didn't feel so alone after that night, and things went back to the way they were before the dreams. The time passed quickly in J's room, and M would bring him his pills from time to time. They would acknowledge each other. J would quell his obsession to try and talk to her, and all she would do is clean, and make sure J was taken of. J had almost forgotten about God. He was quite content. J even wrote a poem in a notebook that he kept under his bed.

The Light
The darkest night
Turns into days
Captive of time
Each hour dies
The beauty—Sublime
She is my sight

A vision
So perfect in ways
Holds me
Unfree
'Til her beauty—I see
Imprisoned

J thought that M must have found the poem at some point and read it. She began acting quite strangely to him, as if she were upset with him, as if he were to never have such thoughts about her. What did she expect?

Anyway, soon God would come back to speak with J, and it wouldn't matter. In the meantime though, one evening with his pills, M brought J a book, Relativity, by Albert Einstein.

"I remembered how much you used to love physics," she said as she set it down on the nightstand, "before, well, when you met me." M curled her hair with her fingers. "I found this in the entertainment center, behind the VCR, in the bottom cabinet, under the TV. I was getting rid of it, no one ever watches it. You just spend all your time in here. So, anyway, I thought you might like to read it."

"It'd be nice… I mean… You think I could read it out…" J motioned to the door, "out… there."

"Don't be silly, of course you can," M giggled, "I don't even know why you think you have to ask me that." M shrugged her shoulders and turned around walking out of the room. J was mystified as the door bolted behind her. He was confused. J opened the book…

10.

Zeke raced down Kennedy Street on his green Fuji racing bike, circa 1976, passing Mr. McManard's house where he lived. He waved at the young girl that lived across the street and three houses down, away from Beacon Street. She was on her front porch. Her name was Traci. Traci didn't wave back, but looked down at the cigarette that was perched between her lips. She raised a large, squared-off Zippo that was a replica of one from the 30's and lit her cigarette. It was a Marlboro, a Red. The lighter sounded, the shrill rubbing of steel on steel, followed by a loud clank. Traci pulled on her smoke and quickly exhaled, then looked up at Zeke's back as he pedaled down the street, no hands on the handlebars. Another clank and Traci closed the large stainless Zippo.

The lighter was a gift to her, from a guy she knew, and she knew a lot of guys. Engraved on it was a sentence: All this happened, more or less. It was the first sentence of Kurt Vonnegut's Slaughterhouse Five. Below the sentence was inscribed "K. Vonnegut". The shop that etched the phrase had made a mistake and put the quotes around Vonnegut's name. Traci liked the lighter. It seemed to tell the story of her life, in one simple sentence.

Traci was pretty. She was half Vietnamese and half Caucasian. She had long black hair, silky like most oriental women, and a long oval face with big lashes over her dark eyes. Her face came to a point at her nose, it wasn't piquant, more narrow, and it had the slightest bump on it in the center. Her lips were thin, her mouth wide and usually painted some shade of pink, a lighter shade of pink. And though she smoked, she kept her teeth white by frequently using one form of whitener or another. She was tall and thin, but not too thin. She ran everyday. Traci had to keep in shape. She was, though most people didn't know it, an escort, a high-priced prostitute, but she was lonely. On this day, she had just turned twenty-nine three weeks prior.

Traci slipped the lighter into the left back pocket of the tight fitting, royal blue, rayon shorts she was wearing beneath a baggy white t-shirt, and she remembered the guy that gave it to her. She hadn't seen him in about three years, and she didn't know what ever happened to him. He was one of the few guys that she met in her line of work that she actually liked a little. He was about her age, maybe a year or two older. He was dark-complected too, with chestnut brown eyes. He was a little shorter than she was, kind of muscular, and he had his straight, dark hair always pulled back into a ponytail, at least when she knew him. She remembered something odd about him, and being a prostitute she remembered it quite clearly: he had no body hair, not a strand. What was his name? James, Jesse, Jason, John? Traci couldn't recall. Either way, she remembered his strong face, and everyday throughout her topsy-turvy world, she thought of him: All this happened, more or less.

Traci smoked her Marlboro out on the porch of her house, enjoying the blue sky that was covered with clouds in the way that only a morning can be, then she went in. Down the front hall, passing the kitchen on her right, and the living room on the left, not quite to the family room, she went up the stairs to her bedroom. The house was older; the floors were oak, and well kept. The paint job was everywhere immaculate. Her room was on the left at the top of the stairs. There was an empty bedroom next to hers, and beside that was Stephen's room, her roommate. They got along well, but she spent most of her time at hotels.

Traci's room was painted a purplish-blue with mauve or puce trim molding. Her bed was made. It had on it a purple and white quilt. There was a large, fluffy chair in the corner that matched the paint on the walls and the white sheer curtains were tied back, letting in the sunlight. Across from the window, kitty-corner to the bed, next to the large, fluffy chair was a desk. The desk was oak, and painted white, in front of a likewise wooden chair. Traci sat down there, and turned on her laptop computer. It was an HP. She quickly opened up her yahoo account to check her mail. This was how she did business— over the Internet.

Traci scanned through her e-mails. There were twelve she had to read, that had to do with business. Two were kind of scary, she deleted those quickly after she opened them and without thinking about them twice. Two were from somebody who had been tormenting her, some guy that wouldn't leave her alone. She got many of those. Seven were customers who were scheduled to meet her in the next week or so, or who were just saying hi. And one was new. A newbie. He sounded interesting. Traci took about a half hour to answer her mail, check her appointment book, and then she got ready for the day. She was on her way to check into the Marriott about three miles from where she lived. She had a lunch date, and then she was meeting someone else there at around 7:00.

As Traci got out of the shower though, something strange

happened; well, maybe it wasn't so strange, but it was something that didn't happen very often. Traci held her face in her hands and she began to cry. She was lonely, and ahead of her was just another day of using and being used.

Traci wiped the tears from her soft face as she walked, wrapped in a towel, from the bathroom back to her bedroom. She drew a line in crystal on a small mirror next to her computer. She bent over, and insufflated it. It seemed the only way Traci could wash away her misery, her loneliness.

11.

A cool night began to set in on the town of Barkley; cool at least, for August. Out on Beacon Street, in front of the Coffee Pot, a man beat some blues from an old Washburn acoustic. The man was unshaven and dressed in worn clothes, but neither he nor his clothes were dirty. He wore shorts cut off from military fatigues, a plain, solid white t-shirt, and brown leather sandals that made his feet appear large. He also wore black, plastic rimmed glasses. The man's music pleased all who passed by him; and as he segued from his progression of chords to a pentatonic solo in E-minor, he raised his head from his instrument and gazed blindly into the newborn starry sky. And as the heavens turned above him, as the sun made it's way across the opposing world, a string, high E, broke, making the six strings merely five.

A young boy, maybe four years old, dirt on his face and cowlick on his blonde head, pushed a number five soccer ball down the street in front of the man with the guitar who had stopped playing. The small boy was pushing the relatively large ball without much ease. It scarcely went straight, and it stopped after moving two feet, or there-abouts. Determined to make it down the street, the boy pushed the ball with both hands, again and again.

The boy's young mother, who appeared eighteen or nineteen, grabbed the child abruptly as the ball rolled out into busy Beacon Street.

Just then Christine, who had been working at the Pot, exited the coffee shop and immediately spied to the west, a meteor, a shooting star, low in the sky.

Around the corner on Kennedy Street, Zeke, in front of Mr. McManard's saw the same star, and as it disappeared into the black night his attention was drawn to Traci, leaving her house with the front door left open and getting into her recently leased, shining black Acura parked in her driveway. Traci had a pleasant gait to her as her hips swayed from one side to the other. She was wearing a pink summer dress that was cut low at the top and cut high at the bottom. She was perched atop black sandals with heals. She waved at Zeke, flashed a bleached-white smile, and giggled a little. She thought to herself that Zeke looked like he was in for some trouble that night as he lurked in the shadows of the porch of Mr. McManard's house across the street. She didn't know him well. She thought him handsome. Didn't really care what he did. Zeke certainly didn't know her.

Traci pulled out of her driveway in her Acura, putting the transmission in drive she headed east on Kennedy Street, slowly. Almost instantly there were sirens behind her, and instinctively, without any panic, as she looked into her rear-view mirror, she came to a stop at the side of the two-lane road. She wasn't a hundred yards from her house. The police cruiser sped past topping fifty in the twenty-five mile an hour zone.

About a half mile further down along Kennedy Street, Traci passed two squad cars, lights ablaze, and a rusted, burgundy colored '78 Camaro, taking great care. The driver of the Camaro was legs spread, hands on the hood of one of the police cruisers. He was being searched. The passenger of the car was handcuffed and a female officer was introducing him to the back seat of her patrol car. The man that was already handcuffed was found in possession of not a gram of marijuana, or more appropriately marijuana seeds. Both men were young and black. The system needed to keep its tabs on them.

The full moon rose up from the south and began to appear above the large oak and maple trees that had stood for scores of years in the back of Mr. McManard's small house where Zeke lived. Zeke liked those trees; he liked to watch them at night, blowing in the soft breezes backed by gray skies. Tonight though, Zeke's nerves were at end. He paced around the property until the early hours of the morning smoking Camel Filters. He was burning at least a quarter pack an hour.

On the front porch of the house, Zeke picked up the copy of the Barkley Post that had been lying untouched, unnoticed for nearly four days. Zeke unfolded it, fairly uninterested, still nervous, sweating. In a column on the right side of the paper, on the front page, was told the story of a teenager, a graduate of Barkley High from the year previous; he had joined the Army, was made into a mechanic, and butchered somewhere in the Middle East. The article sought to console the boy's family and friends. But he suffered.

Zeke skimmed several articles and remained uninterested. One article did catch his attention. It even made him grin, though it wasn't news to him. The recently re-elected President of the national chapter of the United Society of Artisans for Wax Museum Dummies (USAWMD) was to make several stops in the Detroit-Metro area, one of which was to be in Barkley, this coming fall. There was a picture of the guy; boy, did he seem in charge.

Zeke threw the paper into the bushes. He told himself that he was the controller of destinies.

Zeke's attention was grabbed by some commotion across the street. Two houses past Traci's an after-hours party had begun. They were getting quite loud. It was 2 o'clock in the morning. Traci's Acura wasn't back yet. A police car drove past heading west this time, and the officer driving waved at Zeke. Zeke headed inside to his basement.

Sitting on his bed, Zeke stared at a box of Remington 30/06 cartridges that had a place on top of his stereo, rubbing his hands together. After about twenty minutes he rose, washed his face, stripped naked, and fighting some acid, quietly fell asleep quivering on top of the sheets on his bed.

12.

At least once a week, and usually twice for that past summer, Christine, the voluptuous girl of almost twenty who still had braces, and worked at The Coffee Pot on Beacon Street in Barkley, made it a point to visit a small, used piano store at the opposite end of town from where the Coffee Pot was on Beacon Street. It had no name, just a sign in front with large, red, stenciled letters that read BUY/SELL USED PIANOS. If you were to travel from the coffee shop past Mr. McManard's house where Zeke lived on Kennedy Street, and keep going for about another three-quarters of a mile or so, you would come to a quiet corner where Kennedy has for decades met Lyndon Ave; a street that was once called Arrowhead Way at a time before Kennedy was even named. Anyway, ever since the time that Arrowhead met that unnamed dirt road that was to become Kennedy one day, there stood the small, four room house that today is this quaint but lively piano shop. Now the shop wasn't lively in the sense that much ever really happened there. It just had the kind of charm that seemed to make the birds sing lovelier, and the flowers seem that much brighter. But inside, for the past twenty years, ever since the home was turned into this place of business that never seemed to raise much interest in anyone, an old lady whose name will never be of consequence to time but nevertheless was Strzed, bought and sold used pianos. She hired herself out too to tune them, she was very skilled.

The old lady never taught a lesson, but sometimes she would play, and in this sense too, she was quite skilled. But usually, she would pass days, even weeks, in relative solitude with her used, well-tuned pianos, and she would read. In what used to be a small bedroom adjacent to the great room where the pianos were displayed, she kept volumes of books. And in a larger room in the back, the lady made her bed. She was sixty-two this very day when Christine, as she liked to do at least once a week, and twice a week this last summer, walked into her shop and sat down at a sonorous black Steinway that had been there since January but had never sold. Christine loved this piano, and she thought that if she had a house of her own, she would buy it. But she didn't.

On this day, the tail end of the dog days of an Indian summer, Christine waltzed into Ms. Strzed's shop, and sat down at the dark, shining piano she so adored. The old lady lifted only one eye from the book she was reading, a novel by Chopin. It was one she had read many times before, but for some reason, this summer, seeing Christine as she did, she was compelled earlier that day to begin reading it again. She thought of Christine as lonely. The old lady straightened the wire frames of her spectacles as she tried not to smile at the pretty, young girl. Christine settled, glanced up for a moment at the gentle yet sturdy woman who was then beginning to look her age, and then took the keys and began to play. Christine couldn't read music from a sheet, but her theory was sound, and she played eloquently. At times she chilled the bones of Ms. Strzed. She mourned for her youth.

Christine played for a few minutes and as she warmed the knuckles in her fingers, and as the sounding board in the baby grand began to resonate with greater and greater intensity, Ms. Strzed removed herself from her novel and fixed her soft gaze on the young Christine. The old woman, a mother, thought of her son. She remembered him when he was about Christine's age, but now, she thought, he would have to be more than thirty. She hadn't seen him in a few years; it had been more than three. He had gone insane at that time. He had just turned twenty-eight. It was a strange time to go insane, he was doing quite well for himself. His name was... and as she thought of her boy's name, tears welled in her eyes. She wondered how he was. She knew that he was alive and actually lived only about a mile from there at the house where she raised him, where she now bought and sold used pianos. The poor boy, she thought, his wife Mary was in denial of his condition, either that or ashamed of him, she was never sure which. And she kept him locked up in his house, sad, never having any company, feeding him drugs dished out to her by a Doctor. Mary had begun having an affair with the MD who she would eventually fall in love with, and he directed her to feed certain drugs to the disillusioned man. Ms. Strzed still remembered her son as a boy.

She recalled the days, those last days of the 70's, when her husband would play with their boy in the yard trying to keep him out of Arrowhead Way. They were never too successful in keeping out of that street. Ms. Strzed, who had begun to stare blankly at the pages of her book, looked gently to the mantelpiece over the fireplace in the great room of that home where she and Christine now were, to where she kept a lone photograph of her late husband. She remembered his dark, chiseled features and his long hair so typical of the seventies. But the hair looked so appropriate on that great man she once took for better or for worse. He was, after all, one-half Iroquois Indian. Both of his grandmothers were descended from that nation. He died of a heart attack while doing cocaine soon after Ronald Reagan was elected to his first term. Ms. Strzed never remarried, and she raised her son by herself. She regretted never taking her husband's name and giving her son that of Strzed, but it was her husband's will. And she blamed herself for what happened to him, her son, soon after he turned twenty-eight. She thought of him often.

Christine finished playing after doing so continuously for more than thirty-five minutes. As she stopped she turned to Ms. Strzed, and the old lady smiled at her kindly, quickly forgetting her sorrows she focused on the lovely girl. They spoke for a few minutes. Christine always asked her old friend about the picture over the fireplace. The girl knew that he was once Ms. Strzed's husband, but the young lady always could tell her host would grow uncomfortable as she would politely change the subject, wondering. She left, always not knowing.

13.

Christine headed out the door of Ms. Strzed's home that was known better to most as "the used piano shop over on Kennedy and Lyndon". She was feeling happy, light, walking on air. The normally grand Steinway sounded gentle that day for some reason. Ms. Strzed had noticed it; the sound had nearly torn her heart from her. Now Christine was nearly skipping down the street, grinning ear to ear, feeling bashful, shy, herself, gentle. The remnants of the sound the piano made echoed still through Christine's head. The sounds, as the young girl who was still only nineteen danced her way down the street, slowly melted into the songs the birds made in the tall oaks above her. And as she kept on down Kennedy Street, and she put the distance between Ms. Strzed's house on the corner of Lyndon and herself, the sounds of the birds grew alarming, and Christine focused quickly on the cars that were passing her occasionally on Kennedy Street They sounded monotone and tired, slowly breathing, in and out. One at a time: a gold Honda Accord, a red Ford Focus, a blue Chevy Camaro convertible…

Meanwhile, unknown to Christine, about a quarter of a mile in front of her now, Zeke for the first time in his life was making small talk with Traci, Barkley's local escort who was so easily available on the internet, for the first time in their lives. Zeke, who normally was void of most emotion and unexcitable, was almost giddy. He was smiling from ear to ear. Traci was turned on. She had always thought he was cute in a very serious sort of way when she saw him there at Mr. McManard's house across the street from the house that was three down from hers.

Traci had been leaving to get cigarettes at the 7-11 over on Beacon Street, when she saw Zeke on the porch of the house where he rented the basement out, his elbows on his knees, his chin in his hands. He was staring at the grass. Traci thought for a second as she saw him there; really, it was more like a minute. She saw him, grabbed the handle of the driver-side door of her Acura, and she stopped abruptly. She shifted her weight to her left side, took a Marlboro Red from a pack she pulled from her small, pink, leather purse. There were two left in the pack. She pinched the filter for a moment and paused as nothing ran through her mind. Then Traci clenched the cigarette between her lips, looked back into her purse, pulled out the large chrome 1930s replica lighter that was engraved with Kurt Vonnegut's quote from Slaughterhouse Five: All this happened, more or less. She thought of John, who had given it to her. Or was his name Jamie, or Jason, or Jessie? She couldn't remember. Then she turned towards where Zeke who was huddled on the porch across Kennedy Street, and she shouted.

"Hey, you OK?" she yelled.

Zeke looked up to the sky not really comprehending what was going on at first. Then he focused on Traci and said, "Me?"

She laughed, "Yeah you, goof! What are you doin' over there?"

Zeke stuttered, trying hard to think of what to do. "Um, nothin'," he finally decided to say.

"Why don't you come over and talk to me for a while. I'm a little bored. I hate being bored." Traci was being honest with him.

So Zeke, beginning to realize what was happening, got up and trotted across Kennedy Street toward the dark-haired Traci. "She's beautiful," he thought to himself, and he felt a little awkward, nervous. He was blushing and his palms were sweaty; a cold sweat which was unusual for August. Miraculously, he made it to where Traci was standing without tripping or otherwise making a fool of himself. She was smiling, her painted lips parted, her eyes narrow. She dangled her car keys at the end of her straight right arm. She held her Marlboro in her left hand. She pulled on it, and slowly exhaled.

Zeke reached for a cigarette of his own, and quickly realized that he left them back on the porch across the street. He turned and looked back to where they were. He couldn't see them. He was confused for a second.

But without thinking Traci asked him, "You smoke?"

"Yeah. But I think I left my..." He felt the pockets of his jeans, which he wore even though it was hot, and he looked around on the ground for some reason in front of him, and at his sides.

"Here ya go." Traci held out a Marlboro for Zeke, "Marlboro OK? It's a Red."

"Yeah, great." Zeke reached for it and putting it in his mouth, he felt around again for something that wasn't there, a lighter.

Traci smiled, amused, and held out the Zippo that was given to her by John, or Jamie, or Jason, and so on, what seemed so long ago.

Zeke, about to open it so he could light the smoke, stopped and read the inscription: All this happened, more or less, and then "K. Vonnegut". Zeke lit the cigarette and handed the lighter back to Traci. "I love Vonnegut," he said. "Took about a year and read a bunch of his books a while back. Maybe ten years ago. Maybe all of 'em."

"I never read any," Traci admitted, "Are they good?"

"Pretty good. I don't know. I was pretty wasted most of the time I was reading 'em," Zeke said before thinking about it. Then he jumped a little and looked at her. He didn't know if she would think bad of him for getting "pretty wasted." He asked quickly, "So what's your name?"

"Traci," she said quietly, almost whispering. She looked down at her feet, "And you?"

"Zeke," and Zeke scowled. He always hated his name.

Traci liked him right away. She thought. Maybe she needed to settle down. And without a second thought she held the Zippo back out to him. "You can have it."

"What? The lighter?" Zeke didn't know what to do. He smiled. He took the lighter from her gently and looked at it more closely. It wasn't often that people gave him anything.

About ten minutes later Christine was making her way toward Traci's driveway on Kennedy Street. She was about fifty yards from Traci and Zeke. They seemed to be saying their goodbyes. She didn't recognize Traci. But suddenly, with a start, she saw Zeke. She noticed the last car pass her with a whoosh, and the birds again began to sing a beautiful melody. She watched Zeke cross the street back to Mr. McManard's house, and Christine followed. She grew excited. Her throat swelled up and she couldn't take her eyes from Zeke as he sat himself back down on the porch at Mr. McManard's. He played with his new lighter. He was happy.

As Christine got close to him, Zeke recognized her right away. Already in a good mood, something he wasn't used to, Zeke called out to her, "Hey you!" and he waved her towards him. Traci had decided to go out to the bar and sped down Kennedy Street toward Beacon. She smiled at Zeke in the process. What could she do? She liked the guy for some reason.

Christine hurried toward Zeke practically skipping. He put his new flame in his pocket and looked at the young girl. For the first time, he was attracted to her curled auburn hair, her soft curvy shape, and even those braces that she wore. That night the two of them made love in the basement of Mr. McManard's house where Zeke lived. It was only the second time Christine had done it, made love that is, and she was never even really sure if she had done it right the first time. Now she really wasn't sure. Zeke distanced himself from the world again the next morning. The two of them seldom saw each other after that. Zeke tried to avoid her from then on. Besides, there was something he had to do.

14.

J cracked open Relativity. He began to read. J didn't remember much about the book at that point, or the theory, though he had studied it before. J peered out the large window that ran nearly from the floor to the ceiling of the front room of the loft. He sat in the large merlot La-Z-Boy in front of the window and was happy. Rarely was he ever upset, but at that moment, he sat in revelry. M had offered him the room for no apparent reason. That morning, she had just unbolted the lock on the door softly, opened it quietly, and after peering in, she sinuously entered. M then got down on her hands and knees and crawled towards J who was lying on the bed. She smiled seductively, and then she exposed her ass to J as her skirt rose above her hips; she reached under the bed, she felt around for something. After a few seconds, she emerged from under where J was lying with the book: Relativity. M had known exactly where she had put it.

"Why don't you read a while?" M prompted as she rose to her feet, waving the book in her hand. Then she tossed Einstein beside J, and she pulled on her black fishnets at the top. She wasn't wearing a garter, and she felt as if the stockings were slipping down a little. Then she stood straight with a huff and smiled at J inquisitively. She placed her hands on her hips. "You can sit out in front of the window. I know you like it out there."

J looked confused as he thought for a moment. He rubbed his forehead, and looked at M, his eyes wide, then he looked at the book, then back at M, then hurriedly, he grabbed Einstein and shuffled past M, his head down, through the door, down the hall and into the burgundy painted front room of his loft with the cherry-wood floors. J scarcely looked around, but he did notice a clock, its pendulum swinging on the wall, behind the chair, next to the large window where he was beginning to make himself comfortable. He shook his head realizing where the chiming had been coming from for what seemed so long now. It had nearly driven him crazy. J folded back the first few pages of the book. He opened Relativity to page one.

J looked at the page without reading any, and then growing quite despondent he cast his gaze out the large window where his loft overlooked a street a couple of blocks from Kennedy. With a start,

J's attention was drawn toward his kitchen. M was approaching him from it through the large dining room. She had a half of a glass of water in her hand. She reached out with a small blue tablet with her other. The pill was almost purple. J set down the book face-open onto a small end table that was standing lonely next to the chair where he sat, keeping its place at page one. He reached up with both hands, took the pill in the fingers of his left hand and gripped the glass in his right. Shutting his eyes, he swallowed the pill down, and then without looking back at M, J picked the book back up and began to read.

After bending eternal, timeless, forces in the gravity of his mind, and after splitting space into two distinct portions of forever, J looked up. He had been reading for nearly eight hours. He had skipped Lorentz's contributions to Einstein's work and in doing so was realizing the full genius of the author of the Theory of Relativity. J was halfway finished with the book. He would finish it completely later that night. M would bring a table lamp out to him, set it on the lonely end table next to him, and plug it in for him. But for the moment he took a break from the brilliant light of Einstein.

J peered out the large window as he rubbed his eyes, not realizing how long he had been reading. Down on the street, in front of the loft where he lived a couple of blocks from Kennedy Street, he saw a young girl. She was curvy, and beautiful. She reminded J a little bit of M, at least the way she looked. She was wiping tears from her eyes. J did not know her but the young girl was Christine.

Christine was roaming the streets of Barkley, looking for nothing. She was thinking about maybe going to see Zeke. She thought of him often but hadn't seen, or heard from him since the day she made herself so comfortable in his studio apartment in the basement of Mr. McManard's house. That had hurt her, but for the moment it was long forgotten. She had just found out that her Johnny, her high school sweetheart, the boy to whom she had given everything of herself for the very fist time, had been killed. After graduating from Barkley High, Johnny had joined the Army. He was made a mechanic. Soon after, he was shipped off somewhere in the Middle East, and now, as Christine had just heard, Johnny was dead. He had been decapitated. Treated no better than an artist would treat a badly deformed wax dummy. Johnny never even understood what he was doing there in the desert as the hooded man slowly cut off his young head. Johnny was eighteen.

So Christine cried. J wondered what such a young, beautiful girl could be so upset about. She never thought the love of her life could have had his head cut off, and soon after, she gave herself freely to a man who would never love her, and would, in fact, within a couple of days, even forget her name. Zeke. Johnny thought of Christine; her turned button nose, her golden-brown curly hair, the way her braces felt on his lips the last time that she had kissed him as the long blade sliced through the tendon, muscle and bone on which his head was mounted. So Christine cried.

J picked his book back up and forgot about Christine. He hadn't seen M all day and he wondered where she had gone off to. Young valet! J finished the book, and kept things in perspective, a dimension of space in flux. It was time. J put down the book as he finished it that night. The clock struck four in the morning. After, he walked down the hall and into his eggshell colored bedroom. There he saw M lying in his bed, asleep. J laid down beside her, nestled her in his arms, and he too fell asleep. Just as he drifted off, M opened her eyes, slipped from the bed, and began to clean.

The room where J liked to read, in front of the large window that looked down over the road that was so close to Kennedy Street, was now, in M's eyes, in ruin. She spent an hour and a quarter vacuuming, straightening, dusting, sweeping, mopping, and she removed the table lamp that she had put on the lonely end table so that J could see, and read. She cleaned with a purpose. It was more compulsive than necessary or dutiful. The cleaning made her blood flow, hot. She cleaned like the house would fall down if she ever stopped. She loved the cleaning, she thought, and also loved what she cleaned. She didn't love J.

J.L.Judd The Revolution Begins

15.

It was getting to be autumn then. Zeke turned another page on his calendar. It was September. He paced around his basement apartment, back and forth a few times. He was a little drunk and dressed only in navy-blue micro-fleece sweatpants. Zeke ran his fingers down a stack of CDs that were in a plastic tower next to his stereo. He didn't see anything he felt like hearing. He walked again, back and fourth, sighing each time he turned directions. Zeke noticed the flowers, in the wooden jar on the dining table in his darkened studio apartment there in the basement of Mr. McManard's house, had died. They were all dried and had begun to crumble onto the heavy, dark, wooden table. Zeke walked over, and he crumbled one of the wilted flowers in his hand, slowly, dropping it in small pieces, adding to the mess on the table. Zeke stopped, and stood, statue-like, thinking for a moment. He stared at the broken flower on the table.

Blank.

He set his gaze deliberately then on the box of 30/06 cartridges across the room on top of the stereo. He hadn't moved them in weeks. Hadn't touched them. Now, he was ready, there was nothing left to think about. Zeke had a job to do. He looked at the calendar on the wall next to the bed, over the nightstand, where the artificial flowers were resting in their plastic vase. Thirty days in September, and October would come and go, quickly. He knew it. November 1 would be the day, the re-elected president of the United Society of Artisans for Wax Museum Dummies would be there, before he knew it, right there in Barkley, right in his sights. He began to slip into that hole, the one he had been in so often the few weeks before. He thought that soon, soon after November 1, a short nine weeks from the very day that he was then living, he would be dead. He would have to die. His job would be finished, and the job, once complete, required that Zeke could live no more. And it was all about to begin.

Zeke slowly walked to the box of bullets where they weighed heavy on the stereo, and he picked them up. After staring at them for weeks now, he finally touched them and their finality. Their Godlike insanity was pushed through his veins with ferocity. His heart pounded in his chest, THUMP – THUMP, again and again, over and over. His head throbbed of adrenaline. Sweat beaded on Zeke's head. The man focused and began to treat it all simply as an illusion. Zeke turned, crossed the room slowly, and quietly placed the box on the dining table next to the wooden jar that was centered there. He disturbed the pile of dried broken flora that colored its top. Time quickly caught up with Zeke again as he did this, and as space started to again clear itself of distortion, and Zeke's conscience cleared. He turned again and walked over to his closet, reached up to the top shelf feeling underneath a small stack of four or five solid-colored, drab, wool sweaters: a dismal rainbow of gray, burgundy, green and blue. He had to make certain it was there, though he already knew. The safe under his bed was empty. The cold, hard rubber of the tube which held the power to begin the revolution, underneath the sweaters, touched the very tips Zeke's outstretched open right hand. Zeke let the tube be. He left it there, and as Zeke collected himself and reflected on what he was about to undertake, he said out loud, under his breath, "So, the revolution begins."

He extracted a small plastic toolbox from the floor of the closet then. He brought it over to the heavy wooden, rectangular dining table where the 30/06 cartridges now held their place atop the broken, dried flowers from the wooden jar in the center of the tabletop. Zeke pulled out the single chair that was accompanying the table. It too was heavy, dark, and wooden. He sat. From the box, Zeke took one cartridge and set the shell up on its end. He opened the toolbox and removed a file, a small metal-file with a wooden handle. Zeke then proceeded to file down the point of the bullet. He filed slowly, deliberately, for around an hour until the pointy nose of the bullet became a circle, three and a half millimeters flat.

Zeke paused his work then, rested. He lit a Camel. The large, chrome Zippo that Traci had given him a few weeks before clanked loudly as he opened the lighter and then closed it. Zeke read the inscription: All this happened, more or less, and then right below "K. Vonnegut". Zeke calmly put some Grateful Dead on the stereo: AOXOMOXOA, he smoked two cigarettes to their filter, and after lighting a third, he quickly put it out. Jerry Garcia and the rest of the band played in the back while Zeke quickly took his spot again at the squared table and resumed his work. He grabbed a small routing tool, fit it with a bit, plugged it in, and Zeke began to drill. He made a hole about one centimeter deep into the now flat circle that tipped the nose of the shell. Zeke then moved over to the closet and removed the black, hard rubber, tube that was about the size of a Plen-T-Pak of gum, and walked it over to where the hollowed out bullet was standing on the table.

Zeke thought. He was about to break open the well-sealed

container. There would be no turning back. Zeke had no protection from the radiation that he was about to expose himself to, and he knew that even if he were not killed completing the task he had at hand, the task that would be complete on November 1 when the re-elected president of the USAWMD came to Barkley, he would soon after contract some type of illness for playing with God: cancer, leukemia, or the like caused from exposure.

Zeke opened the elliptical tube without giving another thought to what he had done, and sifted some of the Plutonium dust into the hollowed point of the bullet. He filled the bullet with the fissile material to the capacity that he had made it to, packing it tight and soldering it closed with a common lead-tin solder.

Zeke repeated that process carefully that night until all the PU-239 had been used. He made four bullets this way. He placed the four shells back into their original box, and carefully placed them on the highest shelf of his closet beside his drab rainbow of wool sweaters. He replaced the box of tools, too, to its place on the floor of the closet, way in the back, against the wall, and Zeke folded a plain white towel on top of the plastic box. He thought it made his closet look neater. He had stolen the towel. Some things never change.

Then Zeke, walking over to his bookshelf, pulled Vonnegut's Slaughterhouse Five from its place, opened it, and began to read.

"All this happened, more or less…" the book began.

"Let the revolution begin." Zeke thought. And he read. He would finish reading it two days next.

16.

J woke up, the clock was striking: one, two, three times. He planted his feet to the side of the bed, looking to his sides, he stood. J noticed his head was remarkably clear. He took three steps over to the eggshell painted door, turned the handle, and he pushed. It was locked. "Everything seems so white," J thought to himself loudly. He turned, surveying the room. Everywhere was a fog. J shook his head gently, and he wiped his brow with his right hand as he turned to take his place back on his bed. Bending down to the floor, he removed a pad and pen from under the edge of the double bed where he had laid down. He turned the green cover and the first few pages until he came to an empty page. J felt around under the bed until his hand touched something that felt like a pen, or a pencil, he wasn't sure. He grabbed it. It was a blue Paper-Mate. J removed the cap and sticking the pen to the pad, he began to draw: a spiral, it grew. The shape started at a point and wound about itself over and over, four, five, six, seven times until J stopped. J looked at the shape. It looked like a vortex seen from the top, a spiral. A hypnotist's wheel. J stared at the shape with a swirling feeling in his gut.

Beginning in his peripheral, space had, at that moment, become cloudy for J. The already dominantly stark white room seemed to become misty. Then in a flash, J's conscious became clear, followed by a perpetual conception of confusion. But, he wasn't confused. At that point, the darkness set in. A dusk set in about the room, and J shivered for a moment with isolated cold. He cast a quick glance to Einstein's work, bound, he had set it on the light oak nightstand next to his bed. He recalled it all.

"Don't you get it?" God shouted in his rough, booming voice from over in the mirror where he quickly appeared. His head was an outline of yellow, gold. His eyes bulged, and the hair drawn on top of his head was curly, and J imagined it must have been coarse and dark.

J threw his gaze over to the mirror.

Again, God shouted, bluntly, looking vaguely at J. "Don't you get it?" He said.

J thought to himself, "Get what? What are you talking about?" J chuckled in his head. God never frightened him, usually. He made J laugh.

"It's Time." Boldly He spoke.

"Time?" J thought to himself. "What are you talking about now? I don't get it." Since God had begun to visit him, J had developed an ease to his inner-monologue. "This is all in my head!" J told himself.

"I realize I'm in your head, you nitwit, but don't try to think too hard there kid, there's a method to my madness. I've got a plan." J felt comfortable when God said this to him. Then confused a bit, he smiled.

God disappeared as quickly as he had come. He was gone, and again J became overcome by a lonesome chill. The darkened room slowly lightened, and the fog, the haze fell back into the room. The three years past that J had now spent captive in that room seemed to him mere moments. J looked around unable to see, unable to focus. The fog was thick. J snapped his head quickly again towards the mirror looking for God. J was cold, frightened.

J concentrated hard on the glass of the mirror. He had walked up to it, and touched it softly with the tips of his fingers. "What is it?" he thought. He saw something. "What is that? What the hell does that say?"

An equation.

It was there in the mirror, as though it had been written before, the room full of steam, and then the steam disappeared, and the mirror had never been cleaned. And now, the mist that had fallen upon this lonesome prison where J had for so long dwelled had brought the relation at which J was then staring to the surface of the silvered-glass, as it so long ago had been written.

J copied what he saw down into the notebook which he had retrieved from on the bed, and J stared at what he had written, this equation.

Then God again appeared to J. "You got it?"

"I think so. Maybe." J thought as he shook his head and looked at the formula intently. "I think so."

"Good!" God boomed, knowing that J understood full well what he had seen. "Well, here's another. There's two theories over there in that book you just read. Just couldn't put it down, could you? Well now you've done it. Here. Take it. Go and tell the world." God spoke to J as if the imprisoned mortal had managed to swindle a great secret from Him. A secret that He had no intention of revealing. "If you can get out!" God laughed as he slowly, faintly disappeared.

J was in an utter state of bewilderment then. He didn't know what to do. Not the first thing. Then, as he looked at the silvered surface of the mirror again, he was once more enlightened. Another equation, a second equation different form the first, written in the spot that the first had been, all in the steam of the glass, showed itself to him. J hurriedly copied down the second equation as he saw it. J thought intently, holding the notebook out at arms length. He glared at the forms that had been so mysteriously placed on the page. He wrote some, a relation here, an analysis there, then a conclusion. J didn't even realize it, but he had never been so clear headed before. The two equations, J thought with brief insanity, they were the special and general theories of relativity written out there, as formulas! So J kept writing and analyzing, and thinking and writing some more. He would pause occasionally and reflect, and then start writing again. He wrote in a mania as he had been reading the night before. The pages in front of him were all that existed. J wrote for sixteen hours without stopping. What he completed was the theory that is here to follow.

Now if you are not interested in physics, science, or relativity. Or why Zeke for some unknown reason has taken it upon himself to go to the trouble of engineering his four bullets in such a strange way, you can skip J's essay that will be next inserted in this book. The story will play out all the same in the end. I must admit, when J first gave me his work and told me his story before I went to visit Zeke, who I was afforded an opportunity to interview just days before his death once I had heard what he had done, and I put two and two together, I thought the paper he wrote, and here to follow, was a bit confusing myself. J was a layman though, so it does never get too technical, and if you read carefully, and closely, you may be able to follow. But like I said, if you do choose to skip what J wrote, the story, as I am telling it, will still play out the same, and the wax museum dummies, like John, will still lose their heads!

17.

A Supplement to Relativity

J...

To the reader,
The theories of the following text could be of great importance. Not only in understanding the physical theory of gravity and the consequent impact on relativity, but also in their possible applications. I have realized that these theories, if correct, should be made known for the good of science. I realize too that technology can be a very powerful thing, and if you do not discard the following theories, I ask you now to take care in the manners in which you apply them. I must admit that I am no engineer however, I do believe the pursuit of science and technology to be a righteous and noble one. I must add that I have been through much in understanding the concepts here to be known, and I ask that you pray to any God that you can believe in that we should all live in goodness and peace.

The Transformation of Newton's Laws
Introduction:

We know that a moving body or frame of reference will simulate a gravitational field, be it in free space or otherwise. According to the general theory of relativity light bends or shifts in space when encountering any gravitational field. We also know that when a mass moving at some velocity is perceived from two different points of view, i.e. within two different reference frames, that the time of that occurrence is displaced. The event, for each point of view, occurs at two different instances. This work will attempt to show how physics, and not merely the mathematical transformation of Lorentz, would compensate for this displacement of time.

One

We know from observation that light is caused to change
in its direction of motion when encountering a gravitational
field. This is noted in Einstein's Relativity as one of the
properties of the general theory of relativity. I must assume
that gravity is then, in turn, a corresponding result of a change
in direction of light. Without light, gravity would not exist. A
change in the direction of motion of light is the fundamental
source of gravity, and thus gravity will in and of itself cause a
change in direction of any light, or electromagnetic wave,
passing through it's field. The force of gravity will stimulate
a change as to how the energy of an electromagnetic wave,
light, is perceived in it's direction of motion, and thus the
energy of light changing in it's direction of motion is
perceived as the force of gravity. The perception of the
direction of motion of light, since it's velocity remains
constant in free space, must therefore be intrinsically
responsible for the conservation of mass and energy. This is
the fundamental theory, as well as the already existing
theories of relativity, that must be now understood in order to
continue here and understand the concepts here to be
disclosed. I say again, we know from observation that light
will stray from it's original direction of motion when
encountering a gravitational field. I must assert then that it is
a phenomenon of not only gravity causing light to diverge in
its direction but that light changing in it's direction is directly
responsible for the forces of gravity. Mass then too would be
dependent upon the existence of an electromagnetic wave and
the time intervals that are required in the conservation
between mass and energy, I will show, must be determined by
changes in the direction of motion of light, judged by its
constant velocity in space, or consequent changes in
gravitational field.

Two

In Relativity Einstein postulates of a gravitational field
being quite possibly one of mere perception. An entity in free
space will experience, if unacted upon, no sensation of
gravity. The same entity however, once in motion within a
frame of reference, will experience a very real sensation of
gravity. Furthermore, the general theory of relativity states

that light will, in essence, bend when encountering any gravitational field. This is the aspect of general relativity that this work will be most concerned with. I assert that the force of gravity is as a result of an electromagnetic wave moving with a varying direction of motion or vector. The theory of special relativity; the theory that a single instance observed from two different frames of reference with different velocities with respect to one another, will be perceived at two different points of time, will also be of great concern. His theory of special relativity must be taken in its entirety to fully understand the work at hand. The most important thing though to remember of it I must state again. When one occurrence is perceived from two different points of view, and one frame of reference is in motion with respect to the other, it is true that this one occurrence is perceived at a different point of time in each of these reference frames. I must now recommend reading Relativity, if the reader has not already done so, before continuing here. Not only to fully comprehend Einstein's theories of special and general relativity, but also to understand his concepts of coordinate systems, most importantly, that of a non-Euclidian, Gaussian coordinate system. It is a highly enlightening book and one that I do not wish to deface.

Three

I must now disclose the foundation of my theories for the transformation of Newton's laws. Hopefully, upon reaching those pages, after this text has been completed, we will be more fully aware of the processes undergone to draw these conclusions:

$$\Delta t \approx \frac{h}{2\pi c^3} \frac{v}{\Delta m} \qquad \Delta r(G) \approx \frac{h}{4\pi^2} \frac{v}{\Delta E}$$

We will find that we can relate the above two equations to the two theories of relativity. The equation t being that of

the special theory of relativity and the equation r(G) being
that of the general theory of relativity. Just by analyzing the
above equations we can draw some very simple conclusions
about how the universe must function.

Four

Let us first deal with the equation

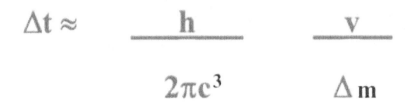

$$\Delta t \approx \frac{h}{2\pi c^3} \qquad \frac{v}{\Delta m}$$

According to this equation, we see that for any reference
frame moving with velocity v with respect to another
reference frame, there must be a change in time t. For a
difference in velocity that is positive, there will be a positive
change in time and vice-versa. From the same relationship, we
can draw the conclusion that for the change in time to be equal
to zero between two reference frames, their velocities with
respect to one another must be zero. We must also draw the
conclusion that the change in mass m between two reference
frames can never be zero. This is a very important property of
this equation and a fundamental concept in the transformation
of Newton's laws when speaking of the theories of relativity.

Here we must admit to supporting the theory of special
relativity: the directly proportional relationship between the
two velocities of two different frames of reference and the
difference in the instance of time that an event actually occurs
for the perceivers within those two reference frames. We must
also draw a new conclusion which I am here casually referring
to as one of the transformations of Newton's laws. We must
admit, according to this equation, the inversely proportional
relationship between the change in time t of an occurrence
observed in two frames of reference and a change in mass m
or corresponding change of energy of the occurrence being

observed. So for an event with a positive change of mass or energy, being observed at two different velocities, there will be a positive time t, with respect to the special theory of relativity after the time interval determined by the Lorentz transformation, when this original mass or energy must be conserved. The reason for this will be dealt with in the next section. Correspondingly, there will be the opposite effect of the change in time t for a negative change in mass or energy. It is important to note here that we are dealing with the mass or energy of the system that is in motion with respect to one observer, and either not in motion, or moving at a different velocity with respect to another. When looking at the magnitude of the constant (Planck's constant divided by twice pi the speed of light cubed) we see also that for there to be any significant change in mass or energy of a system at motion, the velocity of that system must be astronomical when compared to it's change in mass or energy.

So let us assume there is a passing car. There is one observer inside the car, and one standing on the road. Inside the car, a passenger ignites a firecracker. According to the special theory of relativity, this occurrence takes place for the people inside the car before it does for the people along side the road, a difference calculated by the transformation of Lorentz. This is due to the propagation of light and it's constant velocity in space. There is a difference in time of observation of the occurrence by the two observers that can be calculated through a Lorentz transformation. This was supported by the special theory. I assert that if there is a negative change in mass or energy in the system of the moving car with respect to the observer inside the car, caused by the ignition of the firecracker, that there is a conservation of this time which is noticed by the observer along side the road in the form of mass or energy. The result is again, another change of mass or energy in the reference frame of the observer on the ground at the time the change of mass or energy inside the car is noticed by the observer on the ground according to the Lorentz transformation, plus time t. If the firecracker is not noticed by the observer on the ground, there would be no change of mass or energy in his frame of reference. The act of observing is of great importance in the transformation of Newton's laws.

Five

Let us now look at the second equation

$$\Delta r(G) \approx \frac{h}{4\pi^2} \frac{v}{\Delta E}$$

We see here more support for Einstein's theory of
gravity. For if there is a velocity of a system in free space v,
there is a corresponding change r(G) in the direction of the
light passing through the field or frame of reference. It is these
systems, and not those with the Newtonian inclinations of
gravity, i.e. heavenly bodies, that we are primarily concerned
with here. We see too that for any change in mass or energy of
this system there will be corresponding change in the radius of
the gravitational field of that system and thus the direction of
the light passing through it. We know that light passing
through a gravitational field will stray from its "linear"
motion as it passes through that field from the theory of
general relativity as postulated by Einstein. It is the change in
the gravitational field however, stimulated by a change in
mass or energy within a reference frame in motion with
respect to another to which I attribute the change in mass or
energy of the reference frame considered at rest as was
discussed in the previous section. The gravitational field
being changed in the car, the frame of reference in motion
with respect to the observer on the ground, will be observed as
quite a different change in the gravitational field of the same
frame by the observer on the ground as the fire-cracker goes
off. This difference is then conserved by a change in mass or
energy in the frame of reference of the observer on the ground
as was discussed in the previous section. Whether this change
in the frame of reference with respect to the observer on the
ground can or is perceived by the observer in the car, or if it
is solely perceived in the frame on the ground, is not known.

Six

One frame of reference we know must be in motion with respect to the other. Both reference frames should be considered as Gaussian and the time line single and linear. It must be assumed now that a change in mass or energy, where energy is always conserved, occurs. It should be too seen that it must happen at a different velocity within each of these frames. I state again that there still must be at least two observers and that the mass or energy that is changing must be in motion with respect to at least one of these observers. Both still must actually observe the change in mass or energy. As long as these conditions are met the physical spacing of the frames, the size of them, and the distance between them, becomes irrelevant. The reference frame at rest we must now admit does not necessarily require an observer, in which case it extends to infinite and is bounded by the laws of Newton and relativity. However, the resulting change in mass or energy stimulated by the change in the moving reference frame may be forever unnoticed.

Seven

The practical applications of this theory could be phenomenal. We know that the transformations of relativity occur solely at velocities which approach or have reached the speed of light. In Relativity it is said that they could occur as electrons attain sufficient speeds. Working with this new theory however we would find that at the occasion of this occurrence, the electron being released into free space, there would be a conservation of this energy or mass as the electron approaches infinite. As a result there would be a corresponding creation of mass or energy in the frame of reference of a second observer at an appropriate time t always with respect to the transformation of Lorentz. The original velocity of this mass is great with respect to the change in mass of the system and we will find t to be relatively large. However, I assert again that nothing more would happen than an electron appear in the in the frame of reference of the second observer at the appropriate time t. This would be nothing unusual as we know that presently electrons do already roam in free space and have little effect on the everyday observations of the laws of

Newton. At the time that Relativity was written however, two very important concepts of energy did not yet exist. That of a black hole, which I will discuss later in this work, and that of nuclear energy. The concept of fissionable materials and nuclear binding energy we will see next could play a key role in understanding the theory at hand. Let us imagine a bullet which is tipped with a heavy radioisotope, a fissile material. Now let us assume that this bullet impacts an object with sufficient velocity and circumstances so that a nucleus within this radioisotope releases the internal energy. The nucleus would no longer exist as it had; a decay would have been stimulated. However, the "binding energy" (not mass) of the nucleus would have to be conserved. It is energy that has reached the speed of light but now must be conserved as an energy or mass moving at a corresponding velocity, at an appropriate time t corresponding to the observer at rest according to the special theory of relativity and regarding the transformation of Lorentz. This relation t is according to the equation

$$\Delta t \approx \frac{h}{2\pi c^3} \cdot \frac{v}{\Delta m} \qquad \text{or equally...} \qquad \Delta t \approx \frac{h}{2\pi c} \cdot \frac{v}{\Delta E}$$

Since the "binding energy" of this nucleus is relatively large with respect to the velocity of the bullet the ratio of velocity to change in energy is relatively small, as is the constant in the latter of the above equations. Therefore the time interval t would be relatively a short period of time. After the time of the occurrence, as determined by the Lorentz transformation, at a length of time t for the observer at rest, the observer at rest must notice a second energy of approximately equal magnitude to that of the nuclear binding energy traveling with relatively the same velocity as the original nucleus, the original velocity of the bullet. Again, this correction for change in mass or energy is noticed at the appropriate time corresponding to the time interval t with

regards to the Lorentz transformation. I say again that the time interval in the situation described here would be relatively brief and negative, as the change in energy of the system would have as well been negative. The binding energy of the nucleus would reach the point in space corresponding to the impact of the bullet, before the impact of the bullet even occurs. Again, corresponding to a time t.
THIS BULLET, AS DISTINCT MASSES, WOULD IMPACT TWICE.

Cosmo

Eight

We see that a sustained fusion reaction, a star, and the formation of such a body would be a positive change in energy. This body then would be responsible for the change in mass or energy of the future. And it would have this effect when observed "simultaneously" from two points of view. Other than that of a sustained fusion reaction I can scarcely think of good examples to which to attribute a significant positive change in mass or energy. This would be a question for chemistry. Possibly it could relate to the formation of crystals in this sense or maybe the creation of life to a biologist, I do not know. I do however assert here though that the future of physics is in the stars, and I hope I need not say again by the relation aforementioned

$$\Delta t \approx \frac{h}{2\pi c} \qquad \frac{v}{\Delta E}$$

Now, as there motion with respect to one another is
considered we will see that there will be a change in radius of
the gravitational fields surrounding these bodies according to
the equation

$$\Delta r(G) \approx \frac{h}{4\pi^2} \quad \frac{v}{\Delta E}$$

It would be these changes that are responsible for
determining the transformations carried out at the appropriate
corresponding time intervals of t. These changes are never
ending and infinite. Nothing can be done to change it within
this universe, and thus the concept of time travel becomes
more a concept of a parallel universe. We will touch on that
thought again later, but first let us explore the concept of a
black hole. For it is to these changes in gravitational fields of
the heavenly bodies that I must attribute the necessity, and
also the allusiveness, of the black hole.

Nine

A black hole would be a point in space an infinite
distance from us. One that we could always approach yet
never reach. It would be of infinite energy, mass, and
gravitational field at the edge of the universe. It is then, I must
assert, merely light, or an electromagnetic wave moving in a
perfect circle. A concept always unattainable yet constantly
strived for. It is to its infinite amount of energy, and the
correspondingly infinite amounts of energy at the reaches of
space to which you can attribute the circular motion of this
light. I have to believe that they are the only stationary origins
of space in the universe. It can be approached by mass but
never reached. It would be with increasing velocity that a mass
would approach this phenomenon and though never seeming

to pass through it, a parallel universe would be reached. The only change in this universe would be that the mass, in it's approach of this circle of light would seem to disappear, forever.

Ten

As I have stated, as a mass approaches this black hole, it would increase in velocity and seem to disappear to infinite from the universe in which we live. I must assert that at the velocity c/2(pi) (the speed of light over twice pi), the quotient of the two equations at hand, this mass would reach a threshold, a fold of time and space. It would be this threshold too to which the aforementioned physical transformations of this work would be attributed. However if an observer were to reach this velocity, he would again, seem to disappear from this universe. From his point of view though, he would not. He would seem to return, as far as he could tell, to the same universe, however with a different past, and thus a different future. The stars would appear to have moved, he would have reached the time barrier. A new past to him, as well as a new future, yet no longer existing within the universe that we do know.

18.

Zeke headed out on foot from his studio apartment, the basement of Mr. McManard's house on Kennedy Street. He was chain-smoking Camel Filters. Zeke walked for nearly a half an hour. He had made it down to Beacon Street where he turned right, headed north. About a quarter of a mile up Beacon he began to take note of everything. He looked more closely around Barkley than he had ever looked before, at least north of Kennedy. He walked all the way up to the major intersection north of the street where he lived, Beacon and Mile Road. There was a Sunoco station on the eastern corner, across the street form a small Irish pub, O'Mally's. Zeke had eaten there only once. As Zeke stood there, looking across the street into the small bar's parking lot, he saw it was nearly empty. Zeke looked at his watch and he realized it was only two o'clock in the afternoon: not lunchtime, not yet dinner. The overcast of the day had made him think it was later. He remembered the day he had eaten there, at O'Mally's, he saw it was more a restaurant than a bar and since, he hadn't felt compelled to return. Zeke stopped just short of the Sunoco station and looked down into his pack of cigarettes wondering if he needed to buy some. He didn't. He then rubbed the top of his head trying to straighten his thick black hair, and as he squinted his eyes he forced himself to concentrate on why he was there, what he had come to that place a half-mile north of Kennedy Street, on Beacon, to do.

Just before the Sunoco station, Zeke stood in front of the Barkley Federal Credit Union. There was a car pulling out of the drive-thru ATM. That was about as busy as the Credit Union in Barkley ever got. It was a small brown-brick building with no windows. It had no right angles. Across from the Credit Union, Zeke looked, there was a two-story apartment building, Beacon Street Apartments. It was older, not well kept. The building needed paint, and Zeke guessed it was built about fifteen or twenty years earlier. Probably closer to twenty. Next to the apartments, to the south, was the Barkley Public Library. It was small, one story, but tall and made of white masonry, green aluminum trimmed its edges. There were great windows on the majority of its outer walls. And the library too, like the Credit Union, seemed to have no right angles. Next to the library was a vacant lot. The lot wasn't fenced off with flexible, orange, plastic mesh like some vacant lots under construction are, but it was obvious there was, or would be, some type of construction going on there. The green of the grass had been churned into dirt, packed hard, and was brown, some holes dug. A cool wind, one of the first of the autumn, the kind that can only be felt in September in Michigan, chilled Zeke.

A small rent-all was found next to the vacant lot: Chuck's Rent-All, the sign on the building said. There were trailers in the parking lot out in front of it, they were next to industrial backhoes, forklifts, and Caterpillars of all sorts. They were all for rent and the lot was fenced in. The rent-all was on a corner, Kennedy and Willshire. There was a small bar across from Chuck's, across Willshire. There were only two cars in the lot there at the bar. Like the Credit Union, it was about as busy as that bar ever got. Zeke was realizing nothing ever exciting ever really happened in Barkley. He was also realizing that he never really looked so closely at the buildings on Beacon there, north of Willshire, about a half of a mile north of Kennedy where Zeke lived in the small studio apartment in the basement of Mr. McManard's house.

But Zeke was looking around for a reason. He stopped, not finding what he was searching for, and he reflected. He felt as if he had never had a purpose before, and soon he would fulfill all that he was destined to become. He thought about all he was to become and what he had to do, and his heart filled with warmth. He was proud. He told himself softly, in the farthest depths of the back of his brain, that soon, he, Zeke, would be great. He smiled softly, desperately. He clenched his teeth and if anyone would have seen him, Zeke thought, they would thought him to look lost, out of place, and sinister.

Then remembering what he was there to do, the dark man, the shadow of a figure in the overcast afternoon, looked back to the buildings on the side of the street on which he was standing: the Credit Union, Sunoco station, and such. He looked to his left, a small building which housed an insurance salesman along side of a lawyer. And next to that there was a vacant building, large and red. For nearly a year it was a restaurant. The place was a bit too classy for the people of Barkley though. It wasn't overly expensive, maybe a bit, but it was quiet, and dark. Maybe just too pomp for the humble people of Barkley. Either way, it had shut down. Zeke decided there was nothing he was looking for on the side of Beacon Street where he stood, the east side. So more closely then, Zeke peered inquisitively at every window, roof, corner, and door on the other side of Beacon Street. The roof of the apartment building was covered on all sides by trees; there was no clear view of the street. He settled on the roof of the library. Barkley Public Library. He would check it out.

Zeke crossed the street, there was little traffic, and he didn't even need to pause as he looked both ways and darted. He looked in the large window on the east wall of the library and saw a few people inside. No one looked up at him from inside as he approached the building. He shoved his hands deep into the pockets of the tan windbreaker he was wearing and began looking at the building, up and down as he began circling it. A couple of small trees and a few bushes lined the grounds between the library and Beacon Street. There was a large boulder with a copper plaque on it. It read 1994. He turned the northern corner of the building and walked between it and the Beacon Street Apartments. There were a few large oaks. It was dark in the shadows there, but Zeke could see the inside of the library was well lit. There was no one, that he could see, inside that window, and the glass took up nearly the entire side of the structure. Nothing interesting.

Zeke turned the corner and looked around the back of the library. There was a wooden privacy fence that separated it from some modest Barkley houses. And as Zeke moved his glance from the red-stained wooden fence to the wall of the library, behind it, he saw it: a painted black, rusted steel ladder. The ladder was anchored to the white mason wall and Zeke saw there were no windows behind the building. None. There was nothing. Just a large, white cinderblock wall, twenty feet high, and the cold, steel ladder that stretched up to the rooftop.

Zeke continued on. Past the ladder along the blank wall, he peered around the corner to the wall that faced the dusty, vacant lot that stood next to the public library there in Barkley. There was another large window on that wall, it ran the entire height of the structure. Nothing obstructed the view from the roof of the library looking south on Beacon. Zeke grew anxious. Maybe he had found what he was looking for.

Zeke retreated again to the rear of the building and hustled over to where the ladder was. He looked around. There was no one. Zeke reached up and grasped a rung. He pulled himself up, two steps, then three. He looked over the wooden fence behind him, and he saw no one. Zeke scurried up. As he reached the top, he pulled himself up, and he stood, surveying. There was an exhaust fan that was blowing air out from the inside, along with another that was still. And in the center there was a large air-conditioning unit. It too was silent, and it would remain so until the following spring. The surface of the roof was blackened and tarred. Without looking around again, without hesitation, Zeke crossed that roof all the way until he reached the Beacon Street side, and there he perched himself, and he gazed. Zeke looked down onto Beacon Street, for the first time then, from atop the Barkley Public Library. He stared down the barrel of Beacon Street and was overcome again with the smile that anyone else, if they saw him, would call sinister. He clenched his teeth.

Zeke rested. He stared blankly for about five minutes, then, hopping, he crossed the rooftop back to the ladder. He climbed down satisfied, thinking of what may become his legacy to the world, and he headed back to his small studio apartment in the basement of Mr. McManard's house where he stayed there on Kennedy Street.

19.

J had done it. The world as everyone had known it, centuries, had changed. Deep in his heart, in his chest, and in the back of his mind, he had accomplished what he was meant to do. His journey was finally complete, there was nothing left. Nothing left to do. J sat on the edge of his bed, his legs swung off the side, head down, staring at the red and blue specks in the Burbur carpet that was covering the floor. The door opened silently, it didn't creak, it didn't make a sound. M poked her head through the opening, she smiled ambiguously trying to lock eyes with J. She couldn't find them. M surveyed the room. It was bare, nothing out of place; the oak furniture shined, every edge gleamed with light. J tried not to look up as M looked around. She finally focused on the green notebook that sat on the bed next to him. J wasn't wearing a shirt, and he wore red sweat pants that he had cut off just above the knee. White sox bunched around his ankles on his feet. J rubbed his dark hair. M swung open the door and slowly entered. She raised her arms as she traveled a few short steps to the nightstand that was next to the bed. M set down a white saucer there, on it was a small blue capsule, next to that was a half-glass of water.

"Here you go, Sweetie." M said curtly. She straightened her apron, white lace, and she pulled at the bottom of her black skirt and petticoat, then she pulled at the top of her stockings. M smacked her lips together, and then, as she scratched her cheek, she peered inquisitively at J as he raised his head to look at her, his maid.

J squinted, "I don't think I can take that." J took the glass of water, held it to his lips, tilting it. He took a sip. He looked into M's eyes and smiled then as he put the glass back down. He jumped as he noticed the glass nearly fell off the edge of the small table next to him. He caught it, set it firmly on the nightstand, and set his gaze firmly again on M.

M soured, and she stamped her left foot once softly on the carpeted floor. "Take it!" she yelled at J. "I don't know what you've been doing here for the last twenty-four hours! It's that book! I should never have given you that infernal book!" M was yelling, but slowly, she saddened. M began to cry, and she held her face in her hands as she did, and she started to sob.

"I think it's over." J said smugly to M. "I'm gonna have to let you go." J reached into the bottom drawer of the shining nightstand next to his bed. He grabbed a handful of cash, and counted out eight hundred dollars. He handed to the girl who had tormented him for so long now. "Get out, now, please. Here's two weeks pay!"

M took the handful of money, and threw it at J. The money was strewn across the bed; twenties, fifties, hundreds, fell randomly over the bedspread and floor.

"You don't need to be here anymore. You're fired. I love you, but your job is done. There's nothing left here for you to do. I've almost completed everything I was meant for. I have to finish it alone. Now go. Just go! Take care of yourself, Sweetheart. Thanks for everything." J walked out of the room taking M by her hand, and he walked her down the hall through the family room, the dining room, and into the kitchen down the few short steps there to the side door. J looked around as they walked and saw everything shine. There was no dust anywhere. Everything seemed to J to be exactly where it always had been. M sobbed. J opened the door for his maid and watched her bounce as she made her way down the flight of stairs to the street below, the street J had so seldom seen over the last few years, since J had hired M. As the girl walked out through the doorway at the bottom of stairs, and it shut behind her, J heard her sob loudly. She was lost. She was gone. That was the last time J would see her.

J turned around and started to walk back to his room. He noticed things about the loft where he lived then that he had never noticed before. There were plants growing in front of the large windows that shown out to the street in front of his newly claimed second-story home. There were dried flowers in a large brass container, more a bowl than a vase, setting in the center of the small round dining table where M had eaten for years. There were prints on the coffee-colored walls, and a mirrored curio cabinet filled with small brass figurines against the wall in the dining room set away from the family room. J smiled. He stepped into the family room. He lightly glanced around. More plants were in front of that widow, and the green-striped, burgundy couch was clean, vacuumed, like new, as was the burgundy La-Z-Boy that was sitting next to the plants in front of the window, the one that J liked to sit in sometimes when he read, where he had read Relativity. The cherry wood-floors were gleaming. The walls were bare except for the grandmother clock. The pendulum ticked. The lightly stained oak entertainment center that stood high next to the window in that room was shining. There was a small coffee table in front of the couch with a stack of coasters set by themselves in the center of it. J stepped over to them and looked at each one. They contained different pictures: a barrel of apples, a basket of flowers, a phonograph, a teapot, etc. J felt relief, and he walked back into his bedroom.

J picked up the notebook, and opened it. He read what he had written the night before. He read for a half an hour, and he considered carefully every word printed neatly there. Satisfied. J was done. He was complete. He couldn't think of anything else to do. Leaving the book open to its first page on the table next to the bed, J laid down his head. He didn't know if it would be the last time he would do it. The last time he would do anything. J closed his eyes, and he prayed. There was no more God. He was gone. Everything he had imagined, or thought he imagined, was through. One way or another.

For ten hours J would sleep like a baby, and he did not know what he would do when he woke up. He wondered if he could end this, all that he imagined, in such satisfaction. J wondered if everything was right, everything he had written. Could he go any further? His anguish was over now, he thought. He was free. He was free to do what he wished. He hoped he was right.

That night J dreamed, he hated when he dreamed. He woke up in his clean room, alone. He swung his feet off the edge of the bed and rubbed his eyes before standing up. He walked into the hallway, stepping through the family room and into the dining room. He glanced into the kitchen. He was cold. The window, there next to the refrigerator, was gone. There was no pane of glass, no screen, no windowsill, just a bare wood-studded frame. The cold night air blew in. J shivered. He stepped passed the kitchen and into the bathroom. There too, the cold air blew into the room. J turned, back to arch between the dining room and the family room, and there was nothing. The wood flooring was gone. It had been removed. Now it was only covered with green, paint-spattered linoleum. The walls too. Stripped. The plaster was gone. Only studs stood there with fiberglass insulation hanging between them. It was dark, and J was cold. There was a bare bulb hanging from the high ceiling. J had never noticed before how high the ceilings were. All around, it was a gutted home. There was nothing. J stood with his feet rooted in the cold linoleum floor. He screamed. He tried to scream. He raspy voice was nearly inaudible, and J felt as if he were drowning as he tried with all his might to scream. He clenched the muscles in his stomach. Grunts. J tried to yell for M. Her name wouldn't come out. J couldn't move. He just tried to scream. The muscles in his stomach flexed with all the force J could muster.

J woke up in a sweat. He was hyperventilating. He touched himself, his chest, his stomach, his face. He was all there. J took the notebook that was next to him on the nightstand and paged through it until he had passed his work from the day before. He took a pen from near where the notebook had been, and he quickly wrote down the dream, as best as he could remember. He set himself back and wondered to himself how he missed M. He thought of her, his isolation of the last years, and how his life had been nothing but what she had made it: all alone in that bedroom. He closed his eyes again and fell back to sleep, hoping deep in his mind that he would not wake up. His road had ended and there he was, alone, in his empty room.

20.

It was Halloween evening. Zeke painted his face white with black lining his lips and his eyes. He drew in black, too, down his nose. He resembled a skeleton, but that wasn't what he had set out to be. He dressed himself in black, a loose fitting jumpsuit tied at the waist. He was grim. He hoisted a long, thin black sack over his right shoulder. Inside of it, two hours and a half before, just before Zeke had dressed and painted his face, he had put his 30/06. Zeke had spent over an hour the night before pain-stakingly cleaning it. Zeke slipped on a pair of white Reebok tennis shoes, standing, not using his hands. The sneakers showed bright at the bottom of his feet. He grabbed the sack that hung over his right shoulder with his left hand, and after stepping into the bathroom and looking closely at his frightening reflection in the mirror there, Zeke strolled calmly across his small studio apartment there in the basement of Mr. McManard's house.

As dusk set in, Zeke started his walk down Kennedy Street until he got to Beacon. As he walked across the lawn, autumn leaves speckling it, he looked across Kennedy. He saw Traci locking her front door. Zeke hesitated for a second, hoping that after a pause he would have a chance to wave at her. She didn't see Zeke then, and it was the last time Zeke would see her. He made a right and headed north. He crossed over Beacon as he approached where the library was, and ducked around the side of the library between it and the Beacon Street Apartment Building. Zeke passed the great window there, and after seeing no one inside, he looked behind him. Zeke saw nothing, not even a car driving on Beacon. The dark shadow of a man continued to look around as he turned the rear-corner of the library unnoticed. Without looking any further, Zeke concentrated on the ladder that was now in front of him, gripped in his right hand the rung that was level with his eyes, and he pulled tight to his neck the sack which carried the rifle. Zeke climbed deliberately, and as he reached the top he looked down to the ground over his left shoulder. Zeke pulled himself to the roof at the top of the building and walked with care, crouching a little, over to the air conditioning unit that was near the center of the black roof. Zeke slipped the bag off his right shoulder, and kneeling he carefully placed the bag, rifle in it, beneath the air-conditioning unit so as to conceal it as best he could.

Once Zeke was satisfied that the sack was well hidden, and was confident that the next day it would still be there, Zeke looked around and hunched over some, he walked back to the ladder. He turned facing the Kennedy side of the roof and grabbed the top of the ladder in his hands. Then Zeke slipped carefully down. Still, there was silence. Then on the ground, Zeke's heart calmed. He noticed, as it stopped, that the blood had been throbbing in his head. Sweat had started to bead at his hairline and the white paint that was covering his face had begun to ball up on his brow leaving small streaks in their tracks as they slid. He was careful not to touch anywhere on his face where the paint was. He began to notice it all itched. Zeke shook his head, turned to the direction from which he came, first he paused, then he trotted off past the Beacon Street Apartments along the great window on the north side of the library and stopped quickly as he emerged out onto Kennedy Street. He looked around. The street was empty of cars, and there were a few small children dressed to trick-or-treat, bouncing small plastic pumpkins with jack-o-lanterns drawn on them. Zeke righted himself and walked inconspicuously down Beacon Street. He smiled at some of the children that he passed, and he nodded at the adults that walked with them. He said nothing though. At the intersection of Beacon and Kennedy, Zeke crossed the street and he continued to walk south until he got to the Coffee Pot. Zeke stepped in through the door, and through the bustle that was inside. There must have been twenty-five people standing around drinking. They all talked and laughed. There were children running in and out through the crowd of people; they looked like go-carts on a track, weaving and racing. Zeke pushed through the crowd, he looked like sour among the sweet. As he peered through to the counter he saw Christine hurriedly making drinks, her back to all the bustle. A man, his hair dark, thick, and curly like Zeke's, and his skin dark too, took Zeke's order while Zeke stood impatiently. He waited to see if Christine would notice him, but as he waited and she made his hot caramelly cider, Christine only noticed Zeke out of the corner of her eye. She didn't recognize him, his face painted with death.

Zeke took the drink, and forgetting about Christine, he pushed his way back through the twisted mass of people, and the cool rush of autumn night that Zeke felt as he stepped back outside was contrasted on Zeke's lips by the taste of caramel and cider. Calmly, steadily, Zeke made his way back down Beacon Street and turned on Kennedy heading towards Mr. McManard's house. For the first time since he had painted his face that evening, Zeke reached into his front pocket for a lighter and cigarette, and smoked. As he stepped through the kitchen of his studio basement apartment at Mr. McManard's house, and walked through the room with the couch, the bed, and the stereo, and into the bathroom, he turned the switch, grabbed a towel from the counter, and wiped the paint off his face. Smeared, he turned on the shower, removed the loose fitting black jumpsuit, dropped it on the floor, and showered.

After showering, still naked, Zeke went to bed. His mind was empty of what would happen the next day. Still, the whole night Zeke tossed and turned; he dripped with perspiration. The whole of the night he didn't sleep, couldn't. Until the sun came up on that first day of November, Zeke spent a turbulent night, his head void of all that he knew he had to do the next afternoon.

J.L.Judd

21.

J rolled out of bed and stretched tall. He reached for the ceiling. He looked behind him at the mess of sheets and blankets that were atop the bed. J laughed a big, loud, bellowing howl from deep inside his stomach. Then with a grin, J carefully tipped over the half glass of water that was on the lightly stained oak nightstand next to the bed. He grew evermore excited. J grinned, danced and skipped down the hall that led to the wine-colored sitting room where he sometimes liked to read. As he walked, he ran his hands along the walls and he scuffed his feet. When he got to the sitting room he began to throw pillows from their carefully chosen locations all around the floor. J jumped on the green and burgundy striped couch just laughing like a child. Once he had made the biggest, sloppy mess that he could, a ritual that he ended by chanting over and over again, "She's gone! She's gone!" J calmed himself and took a shower.

As J was dressing that morning, the morning happened to be the first day of November, he noticed through the large floor to ceiling window of the room that he had just destroyed that there were people amassing nearly a block away. They were all headed toward Beacon Street. J, excited with the possibility of any interaction, finished dressing and after locking the door to his loft behind him, skipped down the stairs to the street below and headed himself toward Beacon Street. As he got to the street he saw large red, white, and blue banners strung high over the road with people eagerly lined on the sidewalks and curbs of either side. J turned and pushed calmly through the crowd heading north, a direction which took him toward Kennedy Street. He was excited with all the action. J passed right in front of the Coffee Pot as he continued toward Kennedy. He walked all the way until he reached a small vacant building that had at one point been a restaurant, nearly directly across from what appeared to be a small neighborhood bar. There were plenty of people at the bar that day. Something was finally happening in Barkley! J stood there against the front of the vacant building as the loud and happy crowd of people grew in number. They all drank beer and were laughing, and screaming things like, "Bring on the parade!" and, "We're here to see the wax dummies!" J thought that all this was terribly funny.

He stood smiling, waiting for nearly an hour.

Just before noon, the motorcade could be seen making its way down Beacon Street towards the place where J was standing. J looked around, a beaming grin had fallen on his face, ear to ear. He saw the first car. An old, large, black Cadillac convertible headed down the street right towards him. However, J noticed something unusual as the caddy came between himself and the Barkley Public Library that stood across the street. The long, blue barrel of a rifle pointed out off the top of the roof. It followed, slowly, carefully, the Cadillac as it rolled down Beacon. As the car passed J, he froze, not knowing what to do. J couldn't see a face behind the gun, just the brim of a black baseball cap that was concealing a well-groomed head of thick, dark, curly hair. And he saw sunglasses. Large, rounded, black sunglasses.

J then shot a look into the car. There was the re-elected President of the United Society of Artisans for Wax Museum Dummies (USAWMD) waving from the passenger seat. A neatly dressed man in a blue suit who was wearing similar glasses to the man who lay in wait atop the library across the street was driving, and there were two wax dummies riding in the rear. The president's cabinet. Then J looked at the next car in line. Another big, black Cadillac convertible. To J, at that time, it looked like everyone in that car was a wax dummy. Actually, he shook his head, his eyes wide, and it looked like everyone was a wax dummy.

The man that was steadying his rifle on top of the library must have had the re-elected President of the USAWMD in his sights, because right at that moment as J screamed a dry heave from the back of his throat, and the car with the President in it sped up sharply, a Bang! And another Bang! What was happening? Two more shots then and wax was everywhere. Heads exploded. Decapitated, headless wax dummies sped down Beacon Street in their big, black Cadillac convertibles. Their torsos were deathly still. Dummies! And J thought he saw the re-elected President of the USAWMD down in his seat, covered completely in wax, but he wasn't sure.

The crowd was in turmoil. People were running in every direction and J followed suit. He ran, bumping into people, the sight of the gunman haunting him all the way to Kennedy Street. J stopped there and calmed himself. He watched the craziness on the corner of Kennedy and Beacon, a huge, radiant grin on his face. He wiped a bit of wax from his left cheek and looked down at the dirty concrete as he did it. There was some gum stuck to the ground there. That was the last thing he remembered before heading back south where he turned left at his street. He made it back up to his loft and thought blankly for a second or two.

J picked up the phone then. He was happy to find the phone worked and he dialed 911. He explained to the operator everything: what he had seen, where he'd been standing when it all took place. But when the operator asked J pointedly what his name was, and J thought she sounded as if she didn't believe him, J yelled "None of your damn business!" and he slammed the phone back onto its cradle on the wall in the small white kitchen of his loft. It was all over. He ran through his messed loft to his messed room and searched violently for the paper. The work he had done after reading Einstein's Relativity. But it was nowhere to be found. He tossed the mattress over, pulled out drawers and spilled their contents. There was cash everywhere. He couldn't find it. Nowhere. Then at the door. Bang! Bang! "Police, open up." J didn't know what to do. He ran into the small white kitchen of his loft, grabbed a large serrated knife, the first that he saw, and he plunged it deep into his stomach. Blood trickled from his mouth as J tried to pull the knife up towards his ribs. He smiled then as the door on front of him was beaten open. Another Bang!

The police, upon seeing the dying J, immediately called for a medical unit and they tried to dress the wound as best they could. Luckily for me, J would live. He would be all right. He told the police about his paper when they asked why his place had been ransacked. J had trouble explaining the hoards of cash to them though. They retrieved the notebook, and not really understanding any of it they gave it to J as he recovered in the hospital. He was happy. He gave the notebook to me when I came to speak with him about what had happened. He liked me. He thought I was friendly.

Zeke was apprehended later that afternoon in his studio apartment in the basement of Mr. McManard's house on Kennedy Street where he lived. For some reason, the authorities were searching the area for trace amounts of radiation. They found it, and Zeke, there. He granted me an interview from his cell as he waited to be executed. He never made it. He died one year later from exposure to radiation.

That, my friends, was the beginning of the revolution; the one that's been going on for so long now. I'd say years. It gets vocal some times, and occasionally its violence reaches the papers and the evening news, but for the most part it remains quiet. It will continue to spread through the tunnels and underground cells of this phony land. This land of wax dummies, and their artisans, with works like this.

"I finally got those fucking dummies!" I was told that that's all Zeke could mutter, grossly, painfully on his deathbed. It was the last thing anyone heard him say.

J.L.Judd

J.L.Judd

J.L.Judd   The Revolution Begins

J.L.Judd The Revolution Begins